When she stepped inside a deep, husky voice said, "Hello, Paige".

She turned and her gaze connected to that of Jess Outlaw, a cousin to the Westmorelands. A smile touched her lips. "Hello, Jess."

She'd gotten to know him over the years and found that he was someone she felt comfortable with, someone she could relax around. She recalled the first time they'd met over six years ago and how she had been attracted to him the first time their gazes met.

There had been this sensual pull, which was a first for her where a man was concerned. So much so that she'd felt bold enough to do a little shameless flirting.

"You're okay?" he asked her in a gentle and concerned voice.

She leaned back and smiled up at him. Obviously, he'd heard what was being splashed all over the media. "I'm fine. What brings you here from the nation's capital?"

He returned her smile. "I'm here on vacation. Spencer invited me last month when he was in DC, and I decided to take him up on his invite."

"You're going to love it here."

"I do already."

* * *

What Happens on Vacation...
by Brenda Jackson is part of the
Westmoreland Legacy: The Outlaws series.

BRENDA JACKSON

WHAT HAPPENS ON VACATION...

HARLEQUIN

DESIRE

HARLEQUIN®
DESIRE™

Recycling programs
for this product may
not exist in your area.

ISBN-13: 978-1-335-73552-2

What Happens on Vacation...

Copyright © 2022 by Brenda Streater Jackson

This edition published by arrangement with Harlequin Books S.A.

For questions and comments about the quality of this book, please contact us at CustomerService@Harlequin.com.

Harlequin Enterprises ULC
22 Adelaide St. West, 41st Floor
Toronto, Ontario M5H 4E3, Canada
www.Harlequin.com

Printed in U.S.A.

Brenda Jackson is a *New York Times* bestselling author of more than one hundred romance titles. Brenda lives in Jacksonville, Florida, and divides her time between family, writing and traveling. Email Brenda at authorbrendajackson@gmail.com or visit her on her website at brendajackson.net.

Books by Brenda Jackson

Harlequin Desire

The Westmoreland Legacy

The Rancher Returns
His Secret Son
An Honorable Seduction
His to Claim
Duty or Desire

Westmoreland Legacy: The Outlaws

The Wife He Needs
The Marriage He Demands
What He Wants for Christmas
What Happens on Vacation...

Visit her Author Profile page at Harlequin.com, or brendajackson.net, for more titles.

You can also find Brenda Jackson on Facebook, along with other Harlequin Desire authors, at Facebook.com/harlequindesireauthors!

To the man who will always and forever
be the love of my life, Gerald Jackson Sr.
My hero. My heart. My soul. My everything.

To my sons, Gerald Jr. and Brandon.
You guys are the greatest and continue
to make your parents proud.

To my readers who enjoy reading about
the Westmorelands and their cousins, the Outlaws.
This one is for you!

Remember ye not the former things,
neither consider the things of old.

—*Isaiah* 43:18

One

"You're not coming home to Fairbanks during the monthlong summer break in the Senate, Jess?"

Senator Jessup Outlaw moved around his bedroom packing while talking to his oldest brother, Garth, on his cell. "No. I met up with Spencer last month when he was in DC on business. Reggie and I joined him one night for drinks." Spencer Westmoreland was their cousin from California who owned a huge vineyard near Napa Valley. Reginald Westmoreland was Spencer's brother and also a fellow senator.

"Spencer invited me to visit him and Chardonnay at the Russell Vineyards. Since many of you are busy right now and will be down there for the anniversary celebration at the end of the month anyway, I decided to accept his invitation."

"What about town hall meetings with your constituents?"

"I held several while home for Sloan's wedding, so I'm good there. Everyone needs a vacation, even senators."

Jess, as he was known to his family and friends, was thirty-eight and a senator for his state of Alaska. He also had four brothers and a sister who kept him busy. All Jess's siblings worked for the family-owned business, Outlaw Freight Lines. He'd worked there as a corporate attorney for over ten years before deciding on a career in politics. Garth had taken over as CEO a few years ago when their father, Bart, had retired, or more specifically, when the company's board had threatened to oust him.

Garth was the oldest sibling, with only a two-year difference in their ages. Garth and his wife, Regan, would soon be flying to Florida to visit his in-laws for the first time since the birth of their son, Garrison, who was born in the spring.

As of last year, Jess's brother Cash, who was two years younger, had made his home in Wyoming on the dude ranch he'd inherited. He was married to Brianna and they had twin sons, Cason and Cannon. Jess's brother Sloan was four years younger and the most recent Outlaw to marry this past June. Sloan and his wife, Leslie, had recently returned from a monthlong honeymoon.

Maverick, Jess's youngest brother, was seven years younger and was on a business trip to Ireland, while Jess's sister, Charm, who was eleven years younger, had made plans to visit the Westmoreland cousins in Atlanta. The only other family member left was their father, Bart. They'd talked a couple of weeks ago and Bart had mentioned that during August he and Charm's mother, Claudia, would be taking a trip to London.

"You're right. All of us have plans to arrive at the Russell Vineyards at the end of the month for the anniversary celebration, so I guess we'll see you then," Garth said.

Spencer and Chardonnay were hosting a seventy-fifth wedding anniversary party for Chardonnay's grandparents, Daniel and Katherine Russell. It was always a fun time whenever the Westmorelands and Outlaws got together.

"Well, enjoy yourself and give Spencer and Chardonnay my regards."

"I will and I'll see everyone at the party."

A short while later, Jess had finished packing and glanced up at the television when a familiar face flashed across the screen. Grabbing the remote, he increased the volume to hear what the reporter was saying.

A week after illicit photos popped up on social media, actor Kemp Pierson and actress Maya Roadie still refuse to comment. It seems they really got into their roles while in New Zealand filming the movie Midnight Heat. *Apparently, they had their own midnight heat going on in spite of Kemp's serious relationship with actress Paige Novak. Ms. Novak, who just wrapped up filming in Japan, was unavailable for comment. In fact, nobody knows her whereabouts...*

Jess flipped off the television and shook his head. If

the allegations against Kemp Pierson were true, then the man was an asshole. No one deserved that type of betrayal. Jess, of all people, should know. Thanks to Ava Sampson, he'd experienced a similar betrayal ten years ago, and he wouldn't wish that sort of heartbreak on his worst enemy.

It just so happened that Paige Novak was the sister of Pam Westmoreland, who was married to his cousin Dillon. Every so often, his and Paige's paths crossed at some Westmoreland family function. She was a very beautiful woman. A woman he'd been attracted to from the first. But he hadn't acted on that attraction because the timing hadn't been right. He'd needed to focus on his campaign. But he could now say that not hooking up with Paige six years ago was a missed opportunity, one he'd come to regret.

If this vacation offered another such opportunity with a beautiful woman, he wouldn't miss it.

Paige Novak turned away from the window when she heard the knock on the door. After crossing the floor, she glanced out the peephole and smiled as she opened the door. "Chardonnay."

"Hi. I'm just checking to see if you want to join us for dinner."

Paige's smile widened. "I'd love to, and I appreciate you and Spencer letting me crash here for a while." This time last week she had been at the airport in Tokyo when she'd gotten a call from a good friend and neighbor letting her know the paparazzi were camped outside her door. It hadn't taken Paige long to find out why.

The affair between Kemp and Maya had been all over social media.

"You don't have to thank us, Paige. You were over-due for a visit anyway," Chardonnay said.

Paige appreciated that, since she'd been at the vine-yards a week already and had worried about overstay-ing her welcome. "I love it here," she said. "I was just looking at the view and thinking it's so beautiful and peaceful."

"Well, you can stay as long as you want. It's nice seeing the guest villas being used."

"Thanks, and I'd love to join everyone for dinner." She enjoyed Spencer's and Chardonnay's company, as well as that of their three children and Chardonnay's grandparents.

"Great. We'll be eating around five."

"Okay. I need to make a few calls. Nadia has been blowing up my phone for some reason, so I need to call her back."

After Chardonnay left, Paige tried calling her younger sister, who had called four times while Paige had been taking a shower. She wondered what the urgency was. When she got Nadia's voice mail, she figured her sister was in a meeting and left a message for Nadia to call her back.

Paige decided to call her sister Jillian to see if per-haps she knew why Nadia had been trying to reach her. Jillian, who was two years older, was a neurosurgeon and working at a hospital in Florida. "Hi, Jill. Do you know why Nadia has been blowing up my phone?"

"I have no idea," Jill said, sounding rushed. "You

might want to check with Pam. I'm due in surgery and will call you back later."

"Okay."

Crossing the room, Paige then sat down on the sofa to call her oldest sister, Pam, who had married Dillon Westmoreland thirteen years ago when Paige had been fifteen. To Paige, Westmoreland Country—a rural area outside Denver where thousands of acres were owned and occupied by the Westmoreland family—was more home to her than the Novak Homestead she and her sisters still owned in Gamble, Wyoming.

Paige had considered going home to Westmoreland Country after leaving Tokyo, but had decided against it. Pam had enough on her plate with a second set of triplets due to be born any day to Dillon's brother Bane and his wife, Crystal. Pam and Dillon would look after the first set of triplets—who would be barely six years old when the new babies were born. Everyone in Westmoreland Country was excited about the births. The last thing Paige wanted was to allow her issues with Kemp to cloud everyone's happiness.

She speed-dialed Pam's number, and not surprisingly, her sister picked up on the first ring. "Paige? The family wants to make sure you're doing okay."

Paige smiled. She'd only called Pam twice since arriving in Napa Valley last week. Although Paige was twenty-eight, she knew her family still worried about her. "Tell everyone I'm doing fine."

"I wish I were there to give you a hug. I don't like that Kemp betrayed you and now the press will keep it front and center until one of you makes a statement about it."

Since Pam had once been an actress herself, she knew how the media worked. "I'm not keeping up with anything on television or social media, so I'm fine," Paige said. And she definitely had no plans to make a statement.

"Have you heard from Kemp?" Pam asked.

Kemp had called last week when the story first broke, and he hadn't bothered to deny the allegations. Instead, he'd said the affair meant nothing, that he and Maya had had a few drinks too many. He apologized for their reckless behavior and wanted to know where Paige was so he could send her flowers. Flowers! He honestly thought flowers would remedy what he'd done.

What bothered Paige more than anything was Kemp's attitude about the whole thing. He honestly expected her to accept his apology and for them to move on like nothing had happened. She had informed him that wouldn't be happening and for him to get on with life because she intended to get on with hers. He'd refused to accept she was breaking up with him and then had the audacity to get upset when she'd refused to tell him where she was.

"I blocked his number," Paige said.

"Well, just so you know, he's called here three times looking for you. Not that we care, but I think he got mad with us for not telling him where you are. I have a feeling he believes what Nadia said."

"Nadia?"

"Yes. Have you talked to her? Has she told you what she did?"

"No. I see I missed several of her calls, but when I called her back, it went to voice mail."

"She's probably in a meeting," Pam said. After graduating from college with an MBA, Nadia had moved back to Gamble, Wyoming, to manage the acting school Pam owned there.

"What did Nadia do, Pam?" Paige could just imagine. Of her sisters, Nadia was the youngest and was known to be outspoken.

"I'd rather Nadia told you herself, Paige."

Paige didn't like the sound of that and was about to say so when she saw another call coming in. It was Nadia. "Well, she'll get her chance, Pam. I have a call from Nadia. I'll talk to you later."

"Okay."

Paige then clicked to the incoming call. "Nadia, what's going on?"

"Have you listened to the news lately?" Nadia asked anxiously.

"No. Why?"

When Nadia paused, Paige then asked, "Nadia, what did you do?"

"Well, several reporters assumed since you weren't in LA or in Westmoreland Country that you were here in Gamble."

"Reporters showed up in Gamble?"

"Yes, and at the Novak Homestead."

"And?"

"And they were parked outside the house when I left for work. They surrounded me, put their mics in my face and tried to get me to tell them where you were."

Paige swallowed. She knew how insistent reporters could be. "Please tell me you didn't tell them."

"Of course I didn't tell them. But one particular reporter got on my last nerve, so I told him something else."

"What?"

"Well, that particular reporter, a real ass, suggested you were somewhere dealing with a broken heart and that maybe the incident had left you needing intervention."

Paige frowned. "That was a cruel thing to say."

"I thought so, too, which is why I said what I did."

"And just what did you say?"

"I told them that we didn't have to check on you because Kemp was the last man on your mind. That you've already moved on and are seeing someone else."

Paige shrugged. That wasn't true, but it didn't sound too bad. At least, she thought that until Nadia added…

"And that the two of you were involved in a hot, romantic entanglement."

"What! A hot, romantic entanglement? Honestly, Nadia," Paige said, wondering how Nadia came up with such a phrase. She had news for her sister. Paige had never been in a hot, romantic entanglement in her entire life. Even Kemp had left a lot to be desired in the romance department. Although Kemp assumed he was fantastic in bed and took her over the moon whenever they'd made love, in truth, she never even came close to reaching the stars.

"Well, that reporter pissed me off, Paige. You were getting ready to kick Kemp to the curb anyway."

Well, at least Nadia hadn't told *that* to the reporter. Paige had confided those plans to her sisters the last time they'd been together, during the holidays. After almost a year without developing feelings for Kemp, she'd planned to end things when they were back together after filming next month. Although she wasn't brokenhearted by Kemp's affair, she felt hurt and betrayed, nonetheless. He had disrespected her in the worst way a man could do to a woman.

"Now it's all over the media that you're dating someone else, and they're trying to find out where you are and who's your new guy. At least they don't know you're hiding out at Russell Vineyards."

Paige rubbed a frustrated hand down her face, wishing Nadia would have just ignored those reporters or given a "no comment."

"First of all, I'm not hiding out here, Nadia."

"Aren't you?"

"No. I'm visiting our cousins-in-law. My filming project is over, and I consider this a vacation."

"Vacation? Right. I bet you haven't left the vineyard to go into town to shop or anything. To me, that's hiding out."

Deciding to end the conversation with Nadia, she said, "I'm having dinner with Spencer, Chardonnay and the family in a few, and I need to get dressed. I'll talk with you later. 'Bye."

She quickly clicked off the phone. Nadia didn't understand that the media was a force to reckon with. Paige didn't see herself as hiding out. She was merely preserving her privacy for as long as she could. She would make an appearance when she was ready, and not because the media felt she should.

In less than an hour, Paige was walking out of the guest villa to head to the main house. The walk wasn't a long one and she enjoyed strolling around Russell Vineyards—three hundred acres of beautiful land in the Napa Valley.

When she got closer to the main house, she saw a car parked out front next to her rental and wondered if Spencer and Chardonnay were having guests for dinner. The door to the house opened, and Russell—Spencer and Chardonnay's sixteen-year-old son—came out to greet her with a huge smile on his face. Chardonnay had warned Paige that Russell was a huge fan, and his mom suspected he had a crush on her.

"Hi, Paige!" he said, coming down the steps to meet her.

"Hi, Russell. Where's Chablis and Daniel?" she asked. She thought Russell Spencer Westmoreland and his younger brother, Daniel Timberlain Westmoreland, were the spitting image of their father, Spencer; whereas their sister, Chablis, looked like her mother. All three—Russell, Daniel and Chablis—had inherited Chardonnay's family trait of beautiful gray eyes.

"Chablis is helping Mom and Grammy with dinner. How was your nap?"

Normally, she took an afternoon nap every day. "It was wonderful. Thanks for asking."

When they reached the door, Russell opened it and stood back as she entered. He had impeccable manners for someone his age.

When she stepped inside, a deep, husky voice said, "Hello, Paige."

She turned and her gaze connected to that of Jess Outlaw, a cousin to the Westmorelands. A smile touched her lips. "Jess."

When she'd seen the car outside, she hadn't known who would be visiting and had hoped it wasn't someone who would recognize her. The last thing she needed was word of her whereabouts getting leaked. But this was Jess and she'd gotten to know him over the years. He was someone she felt comfortable around. She recalled the first time they'd met, over six years ago, and how she had been attracted to him the moment their gazes had met.

There had been a sensual pull, which had been a first for her where a man was concerned. So much so that she'd felt bold enough to do a little flirting. But what woman wouldn't when Jess was tall, handsome and possessed a demanding presence? Definitely swoon-worthy. Regretfully, he hadn't reciprocated the interest.

Leaving Spencer's side, Jess crossed the floor and reached out to give her a hug. "You're okay?" he asked her in a gentle, concerned voice.

She leaned back and smiled up at him. Obviously, he'd heard what was being splashed all over the media. "I'm fine. What brings you from the nation's capital, Senator?"

A warm smile touched his lips. "I'm here on vacation. Spencer invited me last month when he was in DC, and I decided to take him up on his invite."

"You're going to love it here."

"I do already."

At that moment Mrs. Katherine Russell, Chardonnay's grandmother, appeared in the kitchen doorway with a huge smile on her face. "Dinner is ready, everyone."

Jess offered Paige his arm, and she took it as he escorted her into the dining room.

Two

Jess tried not to stare across the dining room table at Paige. Had she felt the same electrical charge that had raced through him when he'd taken her arm? If she had felt anything, she was doing a good job of pretending she hadn't.

In his lifetime he had met numerous beautiful women, but he was convinced Paige was absolutely the most gorgeous. Everything about her was stunning. First there were her sable-brown eyes. Next were her lips. Their shape was perfect and he loved how they could ease into a sexy smile when she was amused or tilt at the corner when she had nothing to say. Every time he looked at them, he couldn't help wondering how they tasted. Just how sweet and delicious would they be in a kiss?

Then there were the rest of her features. High cheekbones and dimples that made her smile even more dynamic. A perfect nose and a glorious mane of dark brown hair. There was no doubt about it—Paige Novak was a knockout. He could see her beauty dazzling any television or movie screen.

He could clearly remember the first time he'd seen her—when he'd arrived in Denver to attend Bailey Westmoreland's wedding to a close Outlaw family friend, Walker Rafferty. Paige had been one of the bridesmaids, and he, like his brothers, had been a groomsman.

The Westmorelands had kicked off the wedding weekend with a huge family get-together two days before the event. Had it really been over six years ago? Due to being in the thick of his campaign for senator, he hadn't officially met the Westmorelands until a couple of months before the wedding. The Outlaws had been invited to join the Westmorelands for Christmas. It had been a time to get acquainted with the cousins he and his siblings hadn't known existed until a private investigator had shown up in Alaska telling them about the Westmorelands and how they shared the same great-grandfather Raphel Westmoreland.

Up until then, they hadn't known their grandfather had been adopted or that Raphel had died not knowing he'd fathered an illegitimate son. The Westmorelands had the proof, but to this day, Jess's father, Bart Outlaw, refused to accept the facts and claimed there was no Westmoreland blood in their veins. As far as Jess and his siblings were concerned, that was a damn sorry claim when the Westmoreland men and the Outlaw men could pass for brothers. Same thing with his sister, Charm, and the five Westmoreland-born women.

Paige hadn't made the trip home for the holidays that year since she'd been in a new version of *The Nutcracker* in Manhattan. The first time Jess had seen her had been that February at the wedding.

He recalled that day when he'd entered Dillon's home and his gaze had connected to hers. There had been instant attraction. When he'd inquired, he'd been told that she wasn't a Westmoreland cousin but one of Dillon's sisters-in-law. Jess had been glad to know they weren't related, especially when he couldn't keep his eyes off her. The short dress she'd been wearing had showcased a gorgeous pair of legs.

The one thing he recalled more than anything else was that she had flirted with him during those three days he'd been in Denver. He'd felt the magnetism whenever their gazes met or when they were within a few feet of each other. However, the attraction could not have come at a worse time due to his Senate campaign.

He would have to admit that Paige had affected him in an unusual way, and the thought of her had stayed with him for a long time. Now, while sitting across the table from her, he couldn't help but wonder—what might have happened if the timing hadn't been so lousy for him back then?

She seemed to be doing fine, just like she'd said when he'd asked. But she was an actress and was probably doing a good job of hiding her pain. There was no way she wasn't torn up over what that asshole of a boyfriend had done, and knowing her business was all over the media had to be another blow. At least she was smiling while Russell, Chablis and Daniel kept things lively.

A few years ago, Spencer had told Jess how he and Chardonnay had met. Spencer, a wealthy tycoon who enjoyed adding businesses to his portfolio, had set his sights on the Russell Vineyards, with plans to turn it into a resort. Spencer had heard of the Russells' financial problems and had intended to take over their property…until he'd seen Chardonnay. The rest, as they say, was history.

Anyone around the couple for any length of time knew how in love they were. Spencer still built his multimillion-dollar resort, but not on Russell land. Instead, it had been built on property he'd acquired ten miles from here. The five-star resort he called Windemere.

"How do you like being in politics, Jess?" Chardonnay's grandmother asked him, bringing him out of his reverie.

He smiled over at the older woman whom everyone called Grammy. "I enjoy it. Never a dull moment. I'm the new kid on the block and just getting my feet wet. However, I was lucky to get assigned to the education committee." He saw that Paige had stopped eating and was listening attentively.

She said, "I've heard about some of the bills your committee is proposing."

He lifted a brow. "You have?"

"Yes. The last time Reggie visited Westmoreland Country I happened to be home. He mentioned how when you arrived in DC, you hit the ground running. He likes the fact that the Westmorelands have two senators in the family."

The conversation then shifted to all the babies who

had been born in the Westmoreland and Outlaw families in the past year. "Delaney gave birth to twin sons and I hear Sheriff Pete Higgins and his wife are expecting," Spencer said. Pete Higgins was a childhood friend of the Westmorelands.

"I heard that as well," Paige replied. "Everyone is excited about Bane and Crystal's second set of triplets. That's a first in the Westmoreland family. They are due to arrive any day now."

"I hear they're all boys," Chardonnay said.

"Yes," Paige said. "I talked to Crystal a few weeks ago and they were still deciding on names."

Chardonnay chuckled. "They said they wanted a large family, so they are definitely getting one."

"How's your mom?" Jess then asked Chardonnay.

"Mom is doing fine. Now that Dad has retired, they're doing a lot of traveling. I talked to her a few days ago when she called from Paris. They'll be arriving two weeks before the anniversary celebration to help out."

Then the topic shifted to the vineyards when Chardonnay's grandfather began explaining to Paige and Jess how the grapes that were planted in early spring were ready to be harvested and turned into wine during the summer months. And Chardonnay served an apple pie that Grammy had baked with glasses of wine from their vineyard.

"It's Russell's night to do dishes," Grammy said when the meal was over.

"But I want to walk Paige back to the villa, Grammy."

Spencer laughed. "I'm sure Paige has appreciated you walking her to the villa these past few days, Russell, but Jess is heading back that way and I'm sure he doesn't mind making sure she gets there safely."

Jess smiled. "Of course I don't mind." He glanced at his watch and saw it was close to eight already. They'd spent three hours eating and talking, but he had enjoyed everyone's company…especially that of Paige. He saw more laughter in her eyes now than he'd seen earlier, and that was good.

A short while later, he stood. "I'm ready to leave whenever you are."

"I'm ready now," she said, smiling over at him.

Both thanked everyone for dinner and then he escorted Paige out the door.

"It's such a beautiful night, isn't it, Jess?" Paige asked, looking up into the sky dotted with stars.

"Yes, it is. I can even smell the grapes. Can you?"

She sniffed the air and laughed. "Most definitely. Last week I saw the equipment crush and ferment the grapes. It was fascinating to watch."

"I bet it was," he said as they strolled along the well-lit path.

"Over dinner you said you would be here awhile," she said when it got quiet between them.

"Yes, the entire month. The Outlaws are all traveling, so there's no one in Alaska. I'll see everyone when they come to the party."

"Do you have any big plans while you're here?" she asked, thinking this was the first time she ever recalled them being alone. All those times she'd seen him in Westmoreland Country, there had been others around.

He glanced over at her and smiled, showing that dimple in his bearded chin. Instantly, a spike of heat caught in the pit of her stomach. The same thing had happened the very first time he'd smiled at her six years ago. There had been a connection, she'd been certain of it, and she had made sure with her flirtation that he'd felt it. Obviously, she'd been wrong, since he'd never acted on it.

"No big plans other than to rest, relax and enjoy the scenery. And the foods in the area. One of the first things I plan to do is get a pizza."

"You like pizza?"

"I love pizza, and I heard there's this place not far from here called Phillippe's that serves the best," he said. "People say you can't come to Napa Valley without trying it, and that it tastes good no matter what kind of wine you drink with it."

She'd heard that, too, from her agent, Maxie, when she'd called to let her know where she was. "I love pizza, too."

She saw Jess was looking at her with a peculiar expression on his face. "Is something wrong?" she asked.

He shrugged massive shoulders. Paige thought the slacks and button-up shirt looked good on him. She would have to admit that whenever she'd seen him over the years, whatever he'd been wearing had fit his body well. "I was just wondering about something," he said.

"About what?"

She saw the teasing glint in his dark eyes when he said, "While driving here from the airport, on the radio I heard what Nadia said to that reporter, and unless I'm missing something or someone, you don't appear to be engaging in a hot, romantic entanglement with anyone."

Paige laughed. "Nadia likes embellishing things. However, part of what she said was true."

"What part?"

"That Kemp and I are no longer together and that I have moved on."

"Does he know that?"

"He knows—trust me. I told him myself. However, I think he's convinced he can change my mind."

"Can he?"

Paige rolled her eyes. "Not in his lifetime or mine."

They walked for a while in silence before he asked, "How long do you plan to stay here?"

She shrugged. "I was going to leave next week. I don't start another film project for a few months, so this is a vacation for me. Spencer and Chardonnay would love for me to stay longer. I just might since I've seen Chardonnay's to-do list for her grandparents' anniversary party. It's rather long and I might help her shorten it some. That might mean I'll be here for the rest of the month, like you."

She didn't want him to get the impression *he* had anything to do with her decision to stay, so she quickly added, "This is a nice place, and Spencer, Chardonnay, the kids and the Russells make it easy to want to hang around. They take pampering to a whole new level."

"I'm glad. You need pampering."

"Thanks, Jess, but honestly, I'm fine. My only regret is that I misjudged Kemp's character," she added.

"It happens to the best of us—trust me."

She tilted her head to look at him. "Has it ever happened to you?"

"Yes. Ten years ago."

Ten years was a long time ago, but she knew heartbreak could last a lifetime for some people. Especially if they'd truly loved that person. She wondered if that was why he was still single, unlike his brothers, who seemed to be getting married every time she turned around. She couldn't help wondering what had happened.

Then, as if he knew her thoughts, he said, "Ava and I met in law school, and we began dating seriously. It was our plan—at least, I'd assumed it was—for us to start thinking about marriage once we graduated. We'd dated for almost a year and had gotten an apartment together. I had to leave school one week to return home due to a family crisis. I was only supposed to be gone two weeks, but came back early."

He didn't say anything for a minute. "I returned and walked in on Ava and another guy in bed. She said that after a few drinks one thing led to another."

Paige shook her head. "Blame it on the alcohol. Would you believe Kemp said the same thing about his affair with Maya? That they'd had one drink too many and things got out of hand."

Jess shoved his hands into his pockets as they continued walking. "The way I saw it then, and the way I see it now, is that we must not have meant a hell of a lot to Ava and Kemp for an overindulgence in liquor to cause them to be unfaithful to us."

"I agree."

They stopped walking when they came to her villa. "This is your guest villa, right?"

"Yes, this is it. Where's yours?"

"Down the path, about twenty feet away. I'm close by if you ever need me for anything."

"Thanks, Jess."

"Good night, Paige, and just remember one thing."

"What?"

"The man who doesn't appreciate you doesn't deserve you."

She nodded. "Thanks for saying that. Good night."

Paige opened the door and went inside. The first thing she did once she had closed the door behind her was draw in a deep breath. Why did Jess have to smell so good? She had picked up the scent of grapes, but she had also picked up the scent of man. The cologne he was wearing was the same one he'd worn the day they'd met and each time their paths crossed since. She didn't know of any other man who wore that particular fragrance. She recalled being so taken with it that she'd come close to asking him the name of it so she could buy Kemp a bottle for Christmas. Paige never did and now she was glad she hadn't. She honestly couldn't imagine that fragrance on any other man. It was uniquely Jess.

She entered the kitchen to make a cup of tea when her cell phone rang. She smiled, recognizing the ringtone. It was the theme music of a popular medical show. "You're up late, Jill."

"I'm on my way home after performing emergency surgery, and I wanted to check on you."

"I hope the surgery went okay," she said.

"It did. Aidan called as I was leaving the hospital to let me know he has dinner all prepared."

"Lucky you." Aidan Westmoreland was Jill's husband and also Dillon's cousin. Paige thought it was cute that two sisters had married cousins. "One day I hope to marry a guy like Aidan."

"And you will. I'm glad that Kemp's infidelity hasn't made you write off men forever."

"It didn't. Besides, you know my relationship with Kemp was coming to an end anyway."

"Yes, but he didn't know that. Having a man cheat on you has to be disappointing, Paige, and I regret you got tied up with a guy who didn't respect you or your feelings."

"I'm not lessening what he did by any means, but at least I wasn't in love with him to suffer a heartbreak along with disappointment. He was someone I thought I could trust."

"Well, I'm getting a kick out of seeing the media's reaction to that rumor Nadia's started."

Paige rolled her eyes. "I still can't believe Nadia did that. I'm hoping it will soon die down."

"Not sure that it will now that Kemp has made a statement."

Paige nearly dropped the teacup. "What? When?"

"A short while ago. I caught it right before leaving the hospital. When a reporter asked him about Nadia's claim that you'd moved on and were already seeing someone else, he said it wasn't true because you loved him and the two of you are still a couple."

She frowned. "Oh, he thinks I love him, does he?

If he thought that, then why did he have an affair with Maya? And that part about us still being a couple is not true and he knows it. I ended things between us."

"Evidently, he didn't believe you. I hate to say it, but his statement makes you look like a woman who would put up with any bullshit a man throws her way in the name of love. Now that he's considered the Hottest Man Alive, he's convinced he's a prize."

"Kemp can believe whatever he wants," Paige said. "I blocked his calls. He can't reach me and doesn't know where I am." Deciding to change the subject, Paige said, "Guess who's here at Russell Vineyards vacationing?"

"Who?"

"Jess Outlaw."

"The Alaskan?"

Paige couldn't help but grin. Although Jess and his brothers were all eye candy, it had been Jess who had wowed her to the point that she had referred to him as The Alaskan whenever she mentioned him to her sisters. Charm had told them he'd been captain of the dogsled race team in high school and college. Jess Outlaw was so ruggedly built she could definitely see him doing that.

"Yes, The Alaskan. He's on a break from the Senate and will be here until the party."

"I remember when you had that crush on him."

Jill would remember that. "That was a long time ago, and it only lasted during the few days he was in Denver. Once he left, it was out of sight and out of mind."

"Well, I recall you flirted with him a lot."

Yes, she had, but he hadn't been interested. "Like I

said, that was a long time ago and nothing came of it. I was twenty-two and didn't know better. Luckily for me, he was older and did know better and didn't take advantage of my naivete."

She and Jill talked for another half hour before they ended the call. As Paige sat down at the table with her tea, she hoped Jill was right, that one day she would find a man deserving of her love, someone she shared romantic chemistry with as well.

In two years, she would be thirty. She loved acting but didn't intend on making it her life's career. She'd even given serious thought to teaching drama at a university. What she needed to do more than thinking about men was get her personal life in order, and getting back with Kemp was not on the list, regardless of what he'd told the media.

Three

The villa was just as warm and cozy as his studio apartment in DC. It was definitely a lot larger. His brothers often teased him about the size of his apartment when he could certainly afford something more spacious. He was, after all, one of those Alaska Outlaws whose family owned a billion-dollar shipping company. However, he'd never been one to flash and flaunt and had known the moment he'd seen the studio apartment it was exactly what he needed.

He didn't require a lot of space. Just as long as he had a bed to sleep in, a bathroom and a desk to work at, he was fine. Since he'd signed up for one of those meal delivery services, his moderate kitchen served him well. And his place was walking distance to the

Metro. Very few people living in and around Dupont Circle had a car. Everything was conveniently located.

What he liked about the two-bedroom guest villa was the decor, earth tones that blended with the environment. The artwork depicted various locations at the vineyards, and the area rugs gave the place a homey appeal.

He flipped on the television to watch the ending of the baseball game before going into the bedroom to undress and put on something more comfortable. After changing into a pair of cutoff denims and a T-shirt, he walked to the kitchen to grab a beer out of the refrigerator. Spencer had stocked several bottles of his favorite brand.

Picking up the remote, he then flipped through channels to see if there was anything else worth watching when he came to one of those entertainment channels. He was about to turn the television off when he saw Paige's ex.

Jess turned up the volume in time to hear Kemp Pierson say, "Of course Paige isn't happy about what I did. I was wrong and I've apologized. We both agree what I did was a mistake, but not anything we can't work out."

Another reporter then asked, "And what about her sister's claim that Miss Novak has broken things off with you and has moved on?"

A smile spread across Pierson's lips as if such a thing was absurd. "Paige loves me, and regardless of what her sister is saying, there is no doubt in my mind that Paige has not moved on and the two of us will work things out." Pierson then pushed his way through a set of double glass doors.

One reporter looked at the camera and said, "Well, there you have it. According to Kemp Pierson, regardless of his affair with Maya Roadie, he and Miss Novak are still an item."

Jess frowned. Did Kemp Pierson honestly think he could betray Paige the way he had and then appear on national television and say she would forgive him because she loved him? What an ass.

He'd heard enough. He flipped off the television and went to the screened patio out back. The scent of grapes was even more potent here and he noticed his patio faced the one attached to Paige's villa.

After the first time they'd met, whenever his and Paige's paths crossed at any family functions, their encounters were brief and friendly. After he'd won the seat in the Senate and had more time, it was Paige who'd been focused on her career. More than once, he'd thought about giving her a call, but kept putting it off.

When he'd finally decided to get her phone number from Charm, his sister had mentioned that Paige was dating one of the sexiest actors in Hollywood and things looked serious. It was then that he'd realized not reciprocating her interest when they'd met had been a missed opportunity on his part.

His phone rang and he recognized the ringtone. It was his brother Sloan. Clicking on, he said, "Yes, Sloan?"

"Have you heard that BS about Paige and that guy she's been dating?"

Jess took a sip of his beer. Over the years, his brothers and sister had made more frequent visits to Westmoreland Country than he had, so they'd gotten to know Paige well. "Yes, I heard. What of it?"

"The man messed around on her. She deserved better than that."

Jess agreed and that was the same thing he'd told Paige. "Yes, she did."

"Well, I hope what Nadia told that reporter is true, and Paige has met another guy and is somewhere enjoying her time with him."

"Why?" he asked, deciding not to mention that Paige was here at the Russell Vineyards, and she wasn't with a man. It was up to her to share her business.

"You've never met Kemp Pierson, but I have. One of my companies invested in a couple of his movies." Sloan's words reminded Jess that in addition to being an executive in their family's shipping business, Sloan had a stake in several other business ventures, including a film production company in LA. "He's arrogant, self-centered and egotistical. I heard he's even worse now since being voted the Hottest Man Alive by that magazine."

"Well, undoubtedly Paige loved him." According to what Pierson had just said in the interview, she still loved him. He sounded pretty damn sure of it.

"And that's what I don't get. Paige is a beautiful woman and can definitely do better."

"Better than the hottest man alive?" he asked, just to see what Sloan would say.

"Looks aren't everything, Jess. None of the Westmorelands like him either. The few times she's brought him to Westmoreland Country, Derringer claims he acted so condescending and patronizing, they counted the hours until he left. Zane even thought they might have one of those contract relationships for publicity. We all agreed that was a possibility."

Jess lifted a brow. "What's a contract relationship?"

"When a couple pretends they're together. Their agents draw up a contract for the charade. It benefits them both."

Hope sprang up inside Jess. "So, all of you think that's what they had? One of those contract deals?"

"We did, but not anymore. Zane asked her about it, and after she had a good laugh, she assured him that was not true. She and Zane have a close relationship, and she would have leveled with him. Even if she'd signed a contract not to tell."

Jess ignored the disappointment he felt. Wanting to change the subject, he asked Sloan how he and Leslie had enjoyed the road-trip part of their honeymoon. The newlyweds had driven from Alaska to the Lower 48 through Canada. When they had reached New York, they'd boarded a private jet to Belize.

"It was great and the road trip was something we've wanted to do since our college days," Sloan said, adding that he and Leslie would be joining everyone for the Russells' anniversary party.

After ending the call with Sloan, Jess finished off his beer and saw the lights go out in Paige's villa. He hoped she got a good night's sleep, and he looked forward to seeing her again tomorrow.

He wouldn't question why.

* * *

Leaving the villa, Paige glanced up at the sky. It was a great day for an early morning jog. A few years ago, to get in the role of a movie about a competitive runner, she had to get in shape for the part by jogging three to five miles a day. Now she made jogging a part of her regular fitness routine. She'd found a couple of paths around the vineyards, and one led to a huge clearing and lake. After jogging for a while, she slowed down to a walk as she took in the picturesque view.

"Good morning, Paige. You're into jogging, too, I see."

She quickly turned to find Jess standing there. Why did the man have to be so darn attractive even while covered in sweat? And his body. OMG! He was standing there shirtless, wearing a pair of running shorts, and every single muscle was hard, solid and well-defined. Her gaze automatically latched on to his broad shoulders, muscular chest and corded forearms. Even his thighs were exquisitely taut.

He'd been running awhile, if his sweat was anything to go by. Her gaze followed one particular drop as it slowly ran down his chest, then moved past his navel to disappear beneath the waistband of his shorts. Dang, but she envied that drop of sweat.

"Paige?"

When he said her name, she realized that not only had she not responded to his comment, but he'd probably noticed her ogling his body. Looking back up to his face, she said, "This morning I'm doing more walking than jogging, Jess. Seems like you've been at it awhile."

"I have," he said, wiping sweat off his forehead. "I got up before sunrise. Normally I jog five miles a day, but since I registered for this year's Rock 'n' Roll marathon in DC, which is in three months, I figure I better get my body in better shape. Now I'm up to seven miles a day."

She honestly couldn't imagine his body in any better shape than it was now. Even his running shorts were perfect for his lean, muscular hips.

"What about you? When did you get into jogging?" he asked.

His question popped into her thoughts, and it was a good thing. She needed to stay focused. "I started jogging for a part in a movie and decided to keep it up. Some days are more challenging than others."

"I feel you."

If only he knew how often she had dreamed of him doing that very thing. He would feel her all over, first with his hands and then his mouth. It was a good thing he couldn't read her mind.

"I'll let you get back to your walk. I need to go shower before I head over to Bruno's for breakfast."

"Bruno's?"

"Yes. It's in town, and according to Spencer and Chardonnay, it's one of the best places for chicken and waffles. Mrs. Russell offered to make me some, but I refused to let her go to the trouble. Besides, I want to check out the area." He paused a moment and said, "I would invite you to join me, but I know you're hanging low for a while."

Yes, she was. "Well, enjoy your breakfast. I'll see you later at dinner."

"And enjoy the rest of your walk, Paige."

And then he was jogging off, and she stood there watching him until he faded from sight. Her heart was still beating fast, overworked at seeing such male fineness. Not all men who thought they had a fabulous-looking body really did, but Jess Outlaw did. Definitely.

An hour later, she had returned to the guest villa. Chardonnay called to see if Paige wanted to join her for breakfast. Her grandparents were out riding the vineyard in one of the golf carts, Spencer had gone to his office at the Windemere Resort, and now that Russell was driving, the kids had gone into town to meet up with friends. School started back in a couple of weeks, and the three were determined to enjoy the remaining days of summer. Chardonnay figured now was a good time to go over the list of things she still needed to do for the anniversary party.

Paige told Chardonnay she could be there after taking a shower. She was headed to the bedroom when her phone rang. "Yes, Nadia?"

"Is it true The Alaskan is there with you?"

Evidently, Nadia had talked to Jill. "Yes, and do you have to shout in my ear?" Paige asked, noting the excitement in her sister's voice. "And to set the record straight, Jess is vacationing here at Russell Vineyards, but he's not *with* me." She felt she needed to clarify that.

"I think that's great."

Paige put her sister on speakerphone as she began undressing for her shower. "And why do you think it's great?"

"Because next to Jess, Kemp is lacking in so many ways."

Paige would agree. "And what does that have to do with anything?"

"Because if anyone saw you and Jess together, they would assume he's the guy who replaced Kemp."

Paige stopped undressing, knowing how her sister's mind worked. "First of all, Jess didn't replace Kemp, and I don't want anyone getting that assumption. Jess and I just happen to be here at the same time on vacation. We are not together that way, and it wouldn't be fair to him for anyone to assume that we are. For all I know, he might have a girlfriend."

"He doesn't. I talked to Maverick and—"

"Whoa. You talked to Maverick?"

"Yes. He called from Ireland last night after meeting a couple vacationing there from Gamble. I recalled the guy graduated from high school with Jillian. Isn't it a small world?"

Seeing her sister was digressing, Paige asked, "Okay, but what made you ask Maverick if Jess had a girlfriend?"

"I asked out of curiosity when he mentioned Jess was vacationing at the Russell Vineyards."

So, Nadia had gotten word about Jess being there from Maverick and not Jill. "And?"

"And I got a great idea, Paige."

Paige knew her sister like a book. "Whatever crazy idea is going through your head, please get rid of it."

"Just hear me out, Paige, please."

Paige released a frustrated sigh. "What is it?"

"I'm sure you've heard Kemp's comment by now. He acts like he has you wrapped around his finger, not to mention he's calling me a liar."

"It was a lie," Paige reminded her sister.

"Yes, but he doesn't know that. A man who is too sure of himself irks the hell out of me, Paige. Besides, we both know you and Kemp haven't slept together in six months, and even then he was shitty in bed."

There were times Paige regretted Nadia and Jill were her confidantes. She could trust them not to share anything she told them, but sometimes she wanted to handle her personal business herself. There was no need to repeat that the reason she and Kemp hadn't shared a bed was because they'd been on the other sides of the world filming. And there was nothing she could add about Kemp's performance in bed because he definitely lacked there and she'd told her sisters that on several occasions.

"Don't worry about what Kemp is saying, Nadia. He'll be the one with egg on his face when we don't get back together," Paige said.

"But what's wrong with him thinking you've already kicked him to the curb for someone else, Paige? You need to do something to deflate his overblown ego."

"The only thing I need to do is ignore Kemp like I'm doing now."

"What you're doing is hiding out, acting like you're too pitiful and embarrassed to show your face because of what he did. You were the victim and not the perpetrator. Kemp's not hiding out. He's in front of the cameras saying you'll get over anything he's done because you love him."

Paige could tell Nadia was really worked up. "I couldn't care less what Kemp says."

"Well, you should care. You have a lot of fans, Paige. Some are young, impressionable women who look up to you. What type of message are you sending by letting Kemp treat you so shabbily? You're basically telling them to take anything a man dishes out and hide out somewhere in shame. No man should get away with what Kemp did."

Paige appreciated her sister getting upset on her behalf, but at that moment she really didn't want to discuss with Nadia something that really wasn't Nadia's business. "Look, Nadia, I need to shower and get dressed."

"Why? All you're doing is hiding out, so why do you care about how you look?"

Paige tilted her head back. Did Nadia honestly see her as a pitiful coward just because she had backed away from a confrontation with the media? "We'll talk later, Nadia. Goodbye."

"'Bye, Paige."

She clicked off the line and tried not to focus on the disappointment she'd heard in Nadia's voice.

"Thanks for offering to help me with the anniversary party," Chardonnay said, handing Paige a list. "Since I know you still want to keep a low profile, the things I put on your list are things you won't have to leave the vineyard to do."

Hiding out...hanging low...keeping a low profile...

She had heard all three terms used today to define her existence. Was she really sending the wrong message to her young female fans like Nadia had claimed? Shouldn't how she handled Kemp be her business and not anyone else's? Didn't she have the right to avoid the media if she wanted to? But then, she knew, as an actress, the media thought it was their business to share whatever went on in her life. She resented Kemp for placing her in such a predicament.

"Paige, are you okay?" Chardonnay asked, placing a gentle hand on hers.

Paige blinked. "Yes, I'm fine. Why do you ask?"

"Because I asked you a question three times and you didn't say anything. It was as if your thoughts were a million miles away."

"Sorry about that. I was just thinking about something my sister said." She smiled over at Chardonnay as she tried perking up a bit. "I'm glad to help you and I will get started today."

"Thanks, and you're sure you're okay?"

"Yes. I've just got a lot on my mind."

Chardonnay nodded. "I caught the comment that Kemp made on television earlier."

Paige released a frustrated sigh. "I didn't see it, but I heard about it. Nadia is upset with me because she thinks I should do something rather than hang out here hiding, as she put it."

Chardonnay nodded again. "Are you not going to make a comment of your own?"

"I don't want to. I wish the media would move on to some other scandal."

"Do you think they will?"

Paige shook her head. "No. At least, not anytime soon. I have a feeling they will milk it for all it's worth."

Chardonnay was quiet for a moment. "I have a feeling whatever decision you make will be the right one, Paige."

Paige wished she had the same feeling, but she didn't.

Four

Later that day, Jess sat in the same spot on the patio where he'd sat the night before and again sipped his beer. He was on his laptop, checking to see what, if anything, was occurring in Washington. Since most politicians had left for the recess, nothing was happening, but he looked anyway.

He heard a sound and glanced over to see Paige walk off her patio onto the courtyard that connected the four villas. He had strolled the area the first day and liked how the courtyard jutted out into several paths. One path led to a huge guest swimming pool and another to a small pond with a fountain. He'd also stumbled upon a glass-enclosed summerhouse that wasn't far away. He'd nearly missed the summerhouse because it was tucked amid vines, ferns and a cluster of oak trees and palms. It had reminded him of a lovers' hideaway.

Paige appeared deep in her thoughts and hadn't even looked his way. He started to make his presence known, but then decided not to in case she wanted a moment of privacy. That was fine with him since he preferred sitting here watching her as the midday sun highlighted her features.

God, she was beautiful. When he'd seen her that morning while out jogging, her hair had been pulled up in a knot. It still was, but now several loose tendrils had fallen around her face. She had changed and was now wearing a pretty printed sundress that showcased her toned arms and legs. When she sat down on the bench that faced the pond, he could see the sadness in her eyes and it tugged at his heart.

He knew Pierson's statement to those reporters had made headlines. He'd made it seem like all that stuff Nadia said about Paige moving on was utter nonsense.

Jess pinched the bridge of his nose, thinking, not for the first time, that the man was an asshole. A part of Jess wished Paige would prove the bastard wrong just for the hell of it. But then, what she did or didn't do was her business and not his.

After closing his laptop, he grabbed it and the empty beer bottle and went inside. He even milled around a few minutes in the kitchen, hoping that when he returned to the patio Paige would be gone. However, when he went back out twenty minutes later, she was still there, sitting in the same spot and with the same gloomy look on her face.

Something tugged deep inside him. Opening the patio door, he then walked along the courtyard toward her. She was so deep in thought that she didn't hear his approach. When she did hear him, she jerked around with her hand braced over her heart.

"Sorry, I didn't mean to scare you, Paige."

"Jess. I thought you had gone into town and wouldn't be back for a while."

There was no need to tell her that staying away had been his original plan, but he'd sat in that restaurant thinking about her. Specifically, just how sexy she'd looked out jogging that morning. After seeing those tabloid headlines, he'd also thought about the hell her ex was putting her through.

"I decided to come back and check email," he said. "Although I'm on vacation, I'm curious to see what's going on in Washington. It's a bad habit of mine, and one I should break."

"Yes, you should. Vacations are time for fun."

He leaned against a tree and shoved his hands into the pockets of his jeans. "True, but habits, good or bad, are hard to break. Any bad habits you want to break?" He saw how her body tensed with his question. She obviously had loved the douchebag to be hurting so badly. But then, hadn't it been the same for him when Ava had dumped him for her ex? He knew Paige's pain because he'd felt it himself.

"Yes, there is a habit I wish I could break. It's one I started when I became an actress."

"Oh, and what habit is that?"

"Being a conformist. In my former life I was a rebel."

He mulled over her response as he recalled how Dillon had once shared that when he and Pam first met, she'd been engaged to marry another man. A man who Pam's three younger sisters—Jill, Paige and Nadia—had disliked immensely, and the three had rebelled. They'd deliberately annoyed Pam's fiancé to drive him away. Jess had found the tale amusing, an example of the rebellious side of a younger Paige.

"Can I ask you something, Paige?"

"Yes."

"Why did you stop being a rebel?"

She didn't say anything at first and then, "Hollywood is no place for rebels if you want to succeed in the industry. Your image is all they care about. You have a PR person who instructs you on every answer and usually your words are scripted. After a while you forget how to speak up for yourself because doing so can be fatal to your career."

"And is that what's happened to you? You gave in to the Hollywood establishment?"

"Yes, pretty much, so I guess it's not really a bad habit but a way of life I've accepted." She then added, "I talked to Maxie, my agent, just before coming out here. She feels it's time for me to make a statement."

"And what does she want you to say?" he asked, as if he had every right to know.

Releasing what he detected as a frustrated sigh, she said, "She feels I should follow Kemp's lead and admit that, although I needed time alone for the past weeks to sort out a few things, Kemp and I are still a couple.

She doesn't think the timing is right for me to admit that we've broken up."

Timing. That was the one word Jess was coming to detest. "Why does she feel that way, considering what he's done?"

"Mainly because Kemp is Hottest Man Alive and being the woman by his side will enhance my career."

He frowned. "Does your career mean more to you than your pride?" he asked, trying to keep his anger in check.

His tone made her switch her gaze from the pond to him. The moment their gazes met, he felt connected to her. And what was really weird was that he felt it on a deep level. Why? He'd never felt that sort of bond with any woman. At least, not since Ava.

She broke eye contact with him, and he wondered if she'd felt the same connection or if he was just imagining the whole thing. Moments later, she looked back at him and said, "No, but Maxie thinks I should agree to work things out with Kemp."

He didn't say anything for a minute. Then he asked her, "Forget about what your agent wants. What is it that you want, Paige?"

"Honestly?"

He nodded. "Yes, honestly."

A rebellious smile touched her lips and she said, "What I really want, Jess, is to do just what Nadia told the media I'm doing. I'd like nothing better than to make a statement that I've moved on and that Kemp and I are not together and that I am seeing someone else."

"If that's what you want to do, then do it."

* * *

Jess's words made Paige's lips twitch in amusement. "News flash, Jess Outlaw. Wanting to do it and actually doing it are two different things."

"Why?"

She studied him as he leaned against the tree with his hands shoved into the pockets of his jeans. She also took note of the rolled-up shirtsleeves that showed a nice set of forearms. When did a man's forearms become such a turn-on for her? Then there were his dark eyes, which were studying her intently and waiting on her response.

"First of all, doing something like that is career suicide. Even so, a part of me would risk it. But the main holdback is because such a guy doesn't exist. There is no man I'm having a 'hot, romantic entanglement' with."

"And what if there was a guy and you were seen with him?" he asked.

She leaned back on her arms as a whimsical smile touched her lips. "Then Kemp would have egg all over his face for being cocky enough to claim that I hadn't moved on. He would really look stupid."

Jess moved away from the tree and came to stand in front of her. He stood so close his jeans touched the material of her dress. Was she imagining things or was heat radiating off him to her? Or was it coming off her to him? Just moments ago, she had imagined a similar heat when their gazes connected, and for a quick moment she was bounced back in time to when they had first met. She could truthfully say that was the first time she'd experienced instant attraction to a man. And with him standing so close, she was realizing the attraction on her part was still there. Possibly even stronger.

"I have another question for you, Paige."

She unconsciously licked her lips, thinking about his. They went well with his stunning eyes, sexy dimple and fabulous forearms…especially the one with the tattoo of a willow ptarmigan, which she knew was the state bird of Alaska. "And what question is that?"

"Are you opposed to making your ex look stupid?"

His question caught her off guard. She laughed because it had made her day. "Trust me—not in the least. However, hiring a man to pretend to be my new boo would mean contacting one of those escort agencies. Since you never know who will sell your secret for a price, I'd rather not."

"I'd rather you didn't as well," he said, smiling. "Not when I know a guy who would do it at no cost."

She lifted a brow. "You do? Who?"

"Me."

Jess took a step back and prepared himself for all the questions he figured were coming. His hands were still tucked in his pockets, otherwise he would have been tempted to pull her up from the bench and wrap his arms around her. And it would not have stopped there. He truly was attracted to her, even when he knew the last thing she needed right now was a man lusting after her. But it just couldn't be helped. He was lusting.

"You?"

Her question meant she'd finally picked up her

dropped jaw. "Yes, me. Is there any reason I wouldn't work?"

Her gaze roamed all over him. Maybe he was imagining it, but he swore he could feel the heat in her eyes move over his lips, eyes and forearms. Then her gaze connected with his and she said, "No, but…"

Not giving her a chance to complete whatever it was she was about to say, he quickly said, "Good, because I'm applying for the job."

She blinked. "You're joking, right?"

"No. Why should I be joking?"

Then she tilted her head to the side and gave him a speculating glare. "Did Nadia put you up to this, Jess?"

He raised a brow. "I haven't spoken to Nadia. Why would you think she put me up to it?"

She continued to hold his gaze as if she expected to catch him in a lie or something. "Because when I spoke with her this morning, she suggested the same thing after finding out you were here from Maverick last night. Of course, I told her that I couldn't ask you to do such a thing."

"Why not?"

She gave him one of those "duh" looks, as if his question was absurd. "First of all, Jess, it would involve pretending to be romantically involved with me. Your name will become connected to mine in the media."

He shrugged. "I don't have a problem with that."

"Why wouldn't you?"

"Why would I?"

He could tell his counterquestion threw her for a minute. She quickly recovered and said, "I think the answer to that would be obvious. For all I know, you might be serious about someone."

"I'm not."

Paige licked her bottom lip and his stomach clenched watching the movement of her tongue. She was thinking and he was lusting. It was a good thing her concentration was on his face and not below the belt or she would see the evidence of his desire for her. Thinking it might be a good time to sit down, he eased to the bench beside her. She quickly scooted over as if to make sure there was a lot of space between them. He was about to tell her that he didn't bite and decided not to. He would definitely want to take a delicious bite of her.

"Well?" he said.

"Well, I can still see where it might cause you unnecessary problems. You're a senator and are expected to retain a stellar reputation."

He tilted his head and grinned. "And you honestly think my reputation will get tarnished getting linked to yours, Paige?"

"Maybe not tarnished but blasted when our connection appears in the news. The media will beat it to death."

"Let them. It wouldn't bother me. You're a single woman and I'm a single man and we're both here on vacation. What happens on vacation is nobody's business."

"The media will make it their business—trust me."

"Then let them. The way I see it, my name linked to yours just might benefit me."

She lifted a brow. "In what way?"

"I'm a young senator and any publicity is good because it gets a camera or mic in my face and I can control the narrative. If nothing else, I'll get national exposure. It will make for interesting conversation back home with my constituents who think, at thirty-eight, I need more of a social life anyway."

Of course, all he'd just said was a bunch of BS. He wasn't looking for publicity, nor did he relish the thought of a camera or mic in his face, and it definitely wasn't a big deal for him to get national exposure. He'd only said those things as a way to convince her that his reputation wouldn't be tarnished if linked to hers.

"I hear what you're saying, Jess, but I'm not sure we can pull off such a thing."

"Sure we can. I would love nothing more than to see egg all over Kemp Pierson's face."

Paige stood and began pacing. Watching her legs in motion was just as affecting as seeing the movement of her tongue on her lips.

She suddenly stopped and looked at him. "I think we need to talk about it some more, Jess."

"We can do that. In fact, I have an idea," he said.

"What?"

"I didn't get a chance to go by Phillippe's Pizza, but Spencer said they deliver. How about we do wine and pizza for dinner in my villa and talk more about it then?"

She held his gaze, and he knew what she needed. Standing, he opened his arms and she walked right into them, and he held her. The air was filled with the scent of grapes, but at that moment he was filled with the scent of her.

More than anything, he wanted to kiss her, but the timing wasn't right. Would it ever be right for them? One day he wouldn't worry about timing where she was concerned. But not today. What she needed today was a hug.

Moments passed before she finally lifted her head from his chest and leaned back to look up at him. She took a deep breath and slowly let it out. "Thanks, Jess. I needed that."

He smiled down at her. "You can get a hug from me anytime." He truly meant it. "So are we on for pizza and wine later?"

She flashed him a smile, one he thought was hot as hell. "Yes, Jess. We're on."

Five

Paige stepped out of the villa and glanced up into the sky. Although the sun had gone down, the area surrounded by oak trees still reflected the daylight hours. That was the one thing she loved about California. It was still awake while most parts of the country had bedded for the night.

As she walked the path to Jess's villa, she was reminded of the English countryside with unspoiled meadows and valleys. The four guest villas were situated in such a way that they had privacy due to large trees, yet at the same time the windows had views of the lush greenery of the fields.

As she walked, one thought kept going through her mind—her and Jess's earlier conversation. He could definitely give Kemp serious competition. Whereas

Kemp had that proverbial handsome Hollywood look, Jess was effortlessly gorgeous with his strong, masculine features and his tall stature. He didn't need that actor appeal because his all-American look worked for him just fine. He didn't have to work hard for his easy charm and masculine charisma because for Jess those things came naturally.

Knowing how Kemp was convinced his dashing good looks were everything, she wondered how he would react if she appeared in public with Jess by her side. Not only would he have egg on his face, he would see he wasn't the only man alive with hot looks.

Kemp was counting on them working things out and getting back together, although she had told him otherwise. What irritated her more than anything was that he felt entitled to a comeback. So did Maxie. Her agent had called again an hour ago to suggest Paige agree to a press conference, and then asked if Paige wanted her to write out the statement. A statement that pretty much backed up what Kemp had said.

It had taken everything within Paige not to tell Maxie where she could take that statement and shove it. Instead, she'd said she hadn't made up her mind yet. Before hanging up the phone, Maxie had reminded her what she stood to lose if she didn't go along with Kemp. She hadn't bothered telling Maxie what she stood to lose if she did. Namely her self-respect. Nadia had the right idea after all, and now was the time for Paige to take a stand.

The one thing she still wasn't sure about was Jess's involvement. The paparazzi could be intense and brutal at times in their pursuit of a story. She was certain he got coverage in Washington, but media coverage of politicians wasn't the same as media coverage of Hollywood celebrities. Was Jess really ready to find out the difference? She needed to be absolutely sure he knew what he was getting into.

Then there was the fact that after all these years she was still attracted to him. If she hadn't been certain of that before, then their time spent together by the pond had definitely made it real to her. Even while having a serious discussion with him, her mind managed to conjure up sexy ideas where he played the leading man in a hot love scene with her as the leading lady.

But she accepted that Jess wasn't interested in her. For that reason, him playing the role of her lover could lead to problems, more on her end than his. Especially if she was to forget it was only acting.

She reached his villa and had lifted her hand to knock when the door was snatched open. "I saw you coming up," he said, moving aside to let her in.

"Oh." He must have been looking out the window.

She entered and glanced around. "Nice place, Jess."

"I think so, too. I'm sure yours is just as nice."

"Even nicer," she said, laughing. "I've got a better view of the vineyards from my kitchen window."

"Well, I happen to like that my back window faces the pond," he said, grinning. "I've ordered the pizza and it's on its way." He looked at his watch. "It should be here in ten minutes."

"Need my help with anything?" she said, following him to the kitchen.

"No, but you can keep me company while I get things set up. Just grab a chair at the island. If you like, you can go ahead and pour the wine," he said, pulling dishes from the cabinets.

"All right," she said, noticing there were several bottles on the island top. "Which one will we open first?"

He turned and raised a brow. "You plan on going through all three?"

"Why not?" she said, chuckling, while lifting a bottle to read the label. "I don't have a job to go to tomorrow. Do you?"

"Nope. We're on vacation and anything can happen," he said, placing a plate of cupcakes on the counter.

"Where did those come from?" she asked excitedly, grabbing for one.

He quickly slid the plate out of her reach. "This is dessert that Grammy Russell made for us when I told her we were making it a pizza-and-wine evening. As you know, dessert is eaten *after* the main meal, Paige."

She tapped her chin a few times. "You sure?"

He smiled. "Positive. Now tell me which wine we'll drink first."

"This one," she said, handing him the bottle to open. "It was the year Pam was born, so I figure it has to be good."

"That will work," he said, opening the bottle and handing it back to her. At that moment there was a knock at the door. "I believe our pizza has arrived."

With slices on their plates, Jess slid in the seat across from Paige at the island. She had poured glasses of wine, and he took a sip to sample her choice. "Hmm. This *is* good."

She took a sip for her herself and smiled. "It is. I've liked every single glass of wine that has come from this vineyard."

"So have I."

He watched her bite into her pizza, and when she closed her eyes and moaned, the sound was a total turn-on. She sounded like a woman satisfied and he wondered what type of moan she made when caught in the throes of an orgasm. "It's delicious?"

"Too delicious," she said. "It's living up to every claim Maxie told me about a pizza from Phillippe."

Adjusting his position in his chair, he said, "You and your sisters are close."

It was a statement more than a question since he knew they were. However, he figured holding a conversation with her was better than getting turned on while watching her eat.

"Yes, we're very close. We have the same father, but Pam has a different mother. Her mother died when she was three, and Dad married my mother, Alma, when Pam was ten. That's when Jillian, Nadia and I came along. Pam is twelve years older than Jill, fourteen years older than me and sixteen years older than Nadia. While growing up, we were one big happy family. Pam has always been the older sister we adored." She paused. "Jill, Nadia and I cried a river of tears when she left for college."

"Did she go far away?" he asked.

Paige chuckled. "You would have thought she had

moved to Mars from the way we carried on. She'd gotten a scholarship to attend UCLA to pursue an acting career. Then a year later, our life changed. Mom got sick and died."

She had stopped eating as if she was recalling that sad period in her life. "Jillian was eight, I was six, and Nadia was four. Pam had talked about dropping out of college to help Dad with us, but he wouldn't let her. But she came home every chance she got. Then a few years later, Dad got sick and died."

"How old were you then?" Jess asked, watching her take a sip of her wine and getting turned on by the way her lips fit on the glass.

"It was a few days before my fifteenth birthday. Pam had come home before Dad died and promised him that she would take care of us and keep us together, and she did. Even when she married Dillon, she took us with her to Westmoreland Country. I think that's why she and Dillon got along so well when they met. They'd both made sacrifices for their families."

After biting into another slice of pizza, she said, "I love how close you and your siblings are, Jess, given all of you have different mothers. I find that amazing."

"All of us, except for Charm, were raised by Bart since we were babies. How Dad managed to get custody of his sons always baffled us while growing up, but the older we got, we knew. I love the old man to death, but he's such a manipulator. Granted, some of our mothers were gold diggers, but in the end, the only thing they got from Bart was a hard way to go."

She nodded. "What about your own mom? Do you remember her?"

He didn't say anything for a minute. His mother was what she was until the day she died. Hell, even after she died. "My mother, Joyce, was the first official gold digger. I don't remember her from my earlier years because she and Dad got a divorce within the first year of marriage. Bart didn't have to take her to court for custody, but he did so anyway to prove a point."

He took a sip of wine. "I was born with a price on my head. She'd asked for a million dollars for me the moment she'd discovered she was pregnant, and he'd agreed. However, she got greedy and asked for twice that much after I was born and that pissed him off. By the time it was over, Dad's team of attorneys made sure she got half of what she'd originally asked for."

"I guess it doesn't pay to be greedy."

"No, especially when you're dealing with Bart Outlaw. But that didn't stop Joyce from taking him to court several times, but she never could get more. She died of cancer a few years ago and planned this elaborate New Orleans funeral for herself, and she made sure Dad got the bill. The cost was close to a million dollars."

"You're kidding, right?"

"No. Bart outright refused to pay and told the funeral directors they could cremate her and toss her ashes in the Mississippi River, for all he cared. I refused to let that happen, so I paid for it out of my trust fund. She was my mother even though she never tried cultivating a relationship with me no matter how many times I reached out to her."

"What sort of funeral costs close to a million dollars?"

"It was one of those New Orleans jazzy funerals done in grand style with a parade, several marching bands, a procession of umbrellas and a horse-drawn carriage motorcade. My brothers and I had never seen anything like it before. It might have been expensive, but it was also an experience. There's nothing like a New Orleans funeral."

"Is that where she was from?"

"Yes. Born and raised. That's probably why I love Cajun and Creole cuisines so much. It's in my blood."

She smiled, nodding. "It's in my blood, too. My mom was born in Louisiana, but left in her teens when her parents divorced. She loved cooking foods with a New Orleans flair. Did your father attend your mother's funeral?"

"No. The only Outlaws who attended were me, my brothers and Charm."

He noticed she didn't ask him about Charm, and he figured that since the two were friends, Paige knew that Charm's mother had been the one woman Bart hadn't married but not for lack of trying. Hell, he was still trying.

They had finished the pizza, were enjoying the cupcakes and had knocked off the first bottle of wine when she looked over at him and said in a teasing voice, "Any chance we're going to get around to discussing the reason I'm here before the sun comes up in the morning? I hadn't counted on a sleepover."

He knew her comment had been meant as a joke,

and he bit back saying that he had no problem if she spent the night. Instead, he broke eye contact with her to look out the window to see it had gotten dark outside. "I guess it's time, but I really enjoyed just sitting here conversing with you, Paige."

Resting her elbows on the island's top, she looked at him and said, "And I enjoyed talking with you, too. But now it's time to get down to business."

Yes, it was. Easing out of the chair, he came around and took her hand. "I think we'll be more comfortable in the living room."

Tingling sensations rushed through Paige at the feel of her hand in Jess's as he walked her from the kitchen to the living room. Once there, he led her over to the sofa and then took the wing-back chair across from her. When he smiled, she nearly melted. That dimple in his chin was going to be her downfall.

Needing to break eye contact with him, she looked toward the kitchen. "We forgot the glasses and the wine."

"No problem. I'll get them."

When he walked to the kitchen, she was fixated on his every movement, especially those masculine thighs in a pair of jeans and the shape of his tush... OMG! She swore her heart took a thump with every step he took. When, with an agility that had her exhaling a deep breath, he leaned over the island to grab the wine bottle and both glasses in one smooth sweep.

As he returned, she noticed their gazes were locked. It was only when he set the wine and glasses on the coffee table in front of her that she broke eye contact with him. She was beginning to think all that sexual chemistry she'd felt earlier today hadn't been one-sided after all.

He eased back in his chair, glanced over at her and smiled. That sexy smile caused a rush of sensual heat to flow through her. "What are you thinking, Paige?"

He honestly didn't want to know her real thoughts right now, so she stated the other thoughts on her mind. "I'm having misgivings about getting you involved, Jess. I'm thinking about just calling a press conference and telling the media that Kemp and I aren't together, and that I have moved on."

He nodded. "And when they ask about Nadia's claim that you've taken up with someone else, what will you say?"

For a moment she felt like she was being coached by an attorney, but then, he *was* an attorney. At least, that had been his profession before entering politics. She nibbled on her bottom lip. "I won't confirm or deny anything."

"By not confirming it, you're basically denying it."

A part of her knew what he said was true, but why did he have to point it out? Drawing in a deep breath, she said, "I'm trying to give you an out, Jess."

"Why?"

"I just don't want you to feel compelled as a family friend to help me out just so I can retain my dignity."

Paige saw his gaze narrow. "First of all, regardless of what you decide to do, there is no threat to your dignity— trust me. You are one hell of a classy woman, Paige. You've handled yourself admirably through this entire thing. As far as I'm concerned, Kemp Pierson is the one looking like an ass. Some women would have been petty or vindictive. Instead, you've kept a low profile for almost two weeks. But…"

She raised a brow. "But what?"

"But the way you want to handle it is making it seem you really aren't moving on. It appears that a part of you wants to leave the door open to take Pierson back."

"That's not true!"

"Are you sure?"

"Of course I'm sure."

"Then prove it. The only way you can is to make it seem you're now interested in someone else. That will seal the deal. There's no reason anyone should question our story. We've known each other for some time. I'm not married, nor am I in a serious relationship with any woman, and you're single and not in a serious relationship either. I'm confident I could play the part of your love interest with no problem, Paige."

Jess leaned forward and asked, "Why are you so against giving me a try?"

His question, spoken in a warm, deep, masculine voice, counteracted the sensuous chills flowing through her. Paige was certain her heart skipped a beat, maybe two, as his penetrating dark eyes held hers. "I'm not against it, Jess. I'm just not as certain as you that we could pull it off."

"I suggest we give it a try and see what happens."

That was what she was afraid of. Giving it a try and *nothing* happening. He wouldn't be any more interested in her now than he had been six years ago. But what he'd said was true. The only way anyone would actually think she had moved on was for her to be seen with someone else.

"Okay, Jess, if you're positive that you really want to do this."

"I'm positive I want to do this, Paige," he said.

She heard so much conviction in his voice that she was tempted to ask why, but then she knew. Jess was a thoughtful guy who did good things for people. That was obvious, with him footing the bill for his mother's funeral when his father would not. Granted, the woman was his mother, but it wasn't as if they'd had a close relationship. That hadn't mattered. He'd done what he thought was the right thing to do. A part of her didn't want to be another "do good" project for him. But it seemed that she would be.

"Fine," she said. "I hope you don't live to regret it, Jess."

A smile spread over his lips. "I can assure you that I won't."

Six

The next morning Jess stepped out of the shower eager to get dressed and take Paige to breakfast. Last night, while finishing up the second bottle of wine, they made their plans. First on the list was to go to breakfast at a restaurant located in Windemere.

They didn't expect to see any members of the press, just people with cell phones who would take pictures to spread across social media. Proof of a Paige Novak sighting would pinpoint her location and the media would be out in full force during dinner. And he and Paige would be ready when they dined later at Sedrick's.

They had agreed to put their plan into motion only after talking it over with Spencer and Chardonnay. Once the media got wind of Paige's location, there was a pos-

sibility they would camp out near the vineyards, convinced they had a story.

That discussion with Spencer and Chardonnay had
come sooner than they'd expected. While walking Paige
back to her villa last night, they'd run into the couple,
out for a late-night stroll. From Chardonnay's swollen
lips, Jess surmised they'd been out doing more than that,
but he had kept those thoughts to himself.

Both Spencer and Chardonnay had seen Kemp's interview and thought the plan was a good idea. Neither
was worried about the vineyards being bombarded with
media. Like his relatives in Westmoreland Country,
Spencer was friends with the local sheriff, and the man
would know how to handle trespassers.

As Jess continued to get dressed, he again thought
how differently things might have gone if the timing
had been right when he and Paige had met six years
ago. A lot of what-ifs were filling his head.

What if when Paige had flirted with him that night,
he'd flirted back? *What if* his mind hadn't been consumed with his campaign and he had given Paige his
full attention? It suddenly occurred to him that after
six years those what-ifs no longer existed. He was no
longer consumed with his campaign and she wasn't in
a relationship with Kemp Pierson.

Now he was dealing with *why not?*

Jess kept smiling while getting dressed. A pretend
courtship with Paige would be easy. For him, there
would be no pretense about it. He intended to wine and
dine her, and what better place than here at the vineyards while they were both on vacation? To Paige, this

might be an act, but for him, starting today, it would be the real thing. He'd been given a second chance and he intended to give it his best shot.

The phone rang and he knew it was a call from Garth. Another thing that he and Paige agreed to do was let the family know what was going on. Most would figure things out anyway since they knew he and Paige weren't romantically involved. That might be the case for his other brothers, but not so much with Garth.

One night while he was home, over drinks, he'd mentioned his interest in Paige to Garth and that he viewed their first meeting as a missed opportunity. Garth had told him that no opportunity was missed with the right strategic planning.

Garth and Regan were still in Florida. Since it had been late on the East Coast by the time Paige had left last night, he'd texted Garth and asked that he call him this morning. "Hello?"

"Yes, Jess, I got your message. What's up?"

It didn't take Jess long to sum up what he and Paige had decided to do and why. "I've always regretted not striking up a relationship with Paige, Garth—now is my chance," he ended his spiel by saying.

"My only warning, Jess, is for you to keep in mind that she's on the rebound, and most rebound relationships don't last."

Jess rubbed his hand down his face. He, of all people, knew that. All he had to do was remember Ava's betrayal. When they'd met, she'd been broken up with her boyfriend for six months. The same boyfriend he had caught her in bed with less than a year later. "I won't forget what happened with Ava, Garth, but this time I plan to be prepared."

"Prepared how?"

"You're not the only one who knows something about strategic planning. Paige isn't looking to get into another serious relationship, and I can respect that. However, I plan to leave a lasting impression on her so when she is ready, she'll know I'm not a bad prospect."

"Sounds like you've pretty much thought this through."

"I have."

"Then I wish you the best, Jess."

"Thanks, Garth."

A short while later, Jess left the guest villa determined that some very interesting things would be happening on his vacation.

"So, there you have it. That's my and Jess's plan," Paige said to Jill and Nadia. She had arranged a group call with them to tell them what was going on.

She could hear clapping in the background and knew it was from Nadia. "I'm glad the real Paige Novak has returned," Nadia said. "The one with a backbone."

Paige rolled her eyes. "My not making a comment before has nothing to do with not having a backbone, Nadia. It's just how things are done in Hollywood if you want to succeed. It's knowing when to pick your battles."

"Well, I just think having your boyfriend mess around on you, admitting he did and pretending it's no big deal is a battle I'll fight any day. There's such a thing as respect."

She knew Nadia was upset on her behalf and she also knew her sister was right. Paige noticed Jill hadn't said anything. "So, what do you think about my and Jess's plan, Jill?"

"I agree with what Nadia said, but not everybody reacts to a given situation the same way. You know how I reacted when I thought Aidan had cheated on me. I didn't confront him or go into a battle mode. I retreated. He would never have discovered why I broke things off with him if you hadn't told him, Paige."

"Which is why I did," Paige said.

"And I thank you for doing so. Because of my past, I can understand why you haven't gone to battle with Kemp, especially when you'd planned to break up with him anyway. However, Kemp didn't know of those plans, so humiliating you publicly and then brushing it off like you'd take him back regardless of his behavior is pretty darn arrogant on his part. I wouldn't let him off easy and you'll be getting him where it will hurt. His pride. But be careful. It's my impression that Kemp is a man who likes having the upper hand. We all know he thinks a lot of himself. More than he should. The only thing that worries me is that he's not ready to let you just walk out of his life for another man."

"He has no choice. Jess and I plan to be convincing."

"That might be the case," Jill continued, "but you heard what your agent told you. Your breakup with Kemp might have an adverse effect on your career. Are you prepared for that?"

Paige nibbled on her bottom lip. She had thought about her career when she'd gone to bed and couldn't sleep. There was a time when her career had meant everything to her because following in Pam's footsteps had always been her dream. But now she was feeling more negatives about being an actress than positives. "Yes, I'm prepared for it."

"Of course she's prepared for it," Nadia said. "Nobody screws over a Novak and comes out smelling like a rose. I'm glad it was Paige and not me, or Kemp would be missing both balls by now."

Ouch. Paige fought back a grin. Nadia intended to be a renegade until the bitter end. She couldn't wait to meet the man her sister would one day fall in love with. The poor guy better walk the straight and narrow or he wouldn't have a chance. "I hate to end this call, but I need to finish dressing. Jess and I are going to breakfast."

"Um, now, that's something else you need to be careful about, Paige," Jill interjected.

"What?"

"You and Jess pretending. What happens if pretending becomes reality? You were all into The Alaskan a few years ago."

"Yes, but need I remind you that he wasn't into me."

"That might have been the case then, but now the two of you will be spending a lot of time together. People change, things happen."

"I agree with Jill," Nadia piped in to say. "Normally what happens on vacation stays on vacation, but in your and Jess's case, the media is going to let all of us know practically everything you're doing."

"And it will all be an act for their benefit while we're

here. The last thing I want is to get seriously involved with any guy right now and that includes Jess. I need space to get myself together."

After ending the call with her sisters, Paige dressed, deciding to wear one of her new sundresses and a pair of sandals, both purchased while she'd been filming in Japan. She stared at her reflection in the vanity mirror, pleased with the results. With just eyeliner and a touch of lipstick, she was good to go. She smiled when she tossed her head, making her hair fall in waves around her shoulders.

Although getting to sleep last night had been hard, after making an important decision regarding her career, she had awakened this morning feeling good. The best she'd felt since the story about Kemp and Maya had broken. Moving on had never felt so great, and she was doing so with Jess.

Well, not exactly, she thought, recalling Jill's warning. She had to remember that no matter what, she and Jess would only be playacting.

When she heard the knock at the door, anticipation ran through her. Grabbing her purse off the bed, she headed for the door. She opened it and saw Jess standing there, all six foot two of him, and immediately thought—not for the first time—that Jess Outlaw was one hot man. Why did he have to look so good? And why did his jeans and shirt fit so perfectly? Just seeing him gave her a tingling sensation all the way to her toes.

And why did he have to flash her such a sexy smile? Dimple in his chin and all.

"Good morning, Paige. Are you ready?"

"Good morning, Jess. Yes, I'm ready."

If only he knew just how ready she was.

Seven

When Jess walked Paige over to the car, it took all his willpower to act unaffected.

The moment she had opened her door, his gaze had taken in her outfit, and then those long, gorgeous legs in a pair of sandals. Her sundress was an array of colors in a soft flowery print. Thin straps covered her toned shoulders and the neckline scooped in a way that hugged her breasts. And the top portion of the dress was backless. When had he started noticing women's clothes? Down to every single detail? Probably when he'd noticed how well Paige wore hers.

"Thanks," she said, when he opened the car door for her.

His gaze sharpened when he saw a flash of thigh as she eased down onto the leather seat. If that sight had nearly knocked the breath out of his lungs, he didn't want to think what effect seeing more would cause. She glanced up at him, probably wondering why he was still standing there and hadn't closed the door. Giving him a warm, questioning smile, she asked, "Is anything wrong?"

He blinked, glad she didn't have a clue about the desire he was feeling. "No. I was just thinking about something," he said, quickly closing the door and walking around the back of the car to get in. No way he could walk around the front, where she might see the state of his arousal.

When he got into the car, her scent filled his nostrils. He glanced over at her as he settled in the seat behind the steering wheel. "You look nice, Paige." That was an understatement. She looked stunning.

"Thanks, and you look nice yourself, Jess. Are you nervous about breakfast?"

"No." There was no need to tell her the reason he wasn't nervous was because he intended to be himself, a man who not only would enjoy her company but who would also enjoy *her* if given the chance. "Are you nervous?"

She shook her head, making the hair framing her face move silkily around her shoulders. "Nope. I'm just treating this as an acting job."

For some reason, he didn't like the sound of that. He merely nodded, started the ignition and backed out of the driveway. "I talked to Garth and told him of our plan. He will tell the others as needed."

Nodding, she said, "And I talked to Pam last night and Jill and Nadia this morning."

"No one tried talking you out of it?"

She chuckled. "No. They didn't like Kemp much anyway and now they like him even less."

There was no need to mention that his siblings who'd met Kemp Pierson hadn't liked him much either. It really hadn't mattered what they liked as long as Paige had been happy. Obviously, she had been, since she and Kemp had been together for almost a year.

"What about Garth?"

Now it was his turn to chuckle. "You know Garth. He has strategic planning down to an art form and thinks it will work. Of course, he said that we have to be convincing." He decided not to tell her what else Garth had said.

"I agree. However, I know how reporters' minds work, so how will we handle it if one comes right out and asks if we've been involved in a 'hot, romantic entanglement'? You just got here a couple of days ago, which could be easily tracked, so how can wc be engaged in something like that already?"

Didn't she know it wasn't uncommon for a romantic relationship to follow after a breakup like hers? But then, like Garth had warned, most of those rebounds didn't last.

"Anything is possible, Paige. We can certainly give off enough chemistry to convince people there's a strong attraction between us." He decided to switch subjects so she wouldn't ask any more questions that he really didn't want to answer. "This is beautiful country, isn't it?"

The sun was out, and the sky was blue. The road they were traveling was high in the valley, and below, as far as the eye could see, were rows and rows of vineyards. Even from their distance, he could see ripe grapes.

"Yes, it is beautiful."

She was beautiful, he thought, glancing over at her. "Tell me about the movie you just completed in Japan. How did it go?"

Paige glanced over at him and smiled. "I think it wrapped up well—at least, my director said it did. He was easy to work with."

He nodded. "Anyone else in it that I might have heard of?"

She answered him but he didn't recognize any names. He wasn't into movies, but he would admit to having watched every single one she'd been in.

"You were the lead, right?" he asked.

"Yes. My first time. One of the reasons Maxie wants me to stay with Kemp is because some big-time producer wants Kemp and I to make a movie together."

"Could you do that after what he did?"

She shrugged. "Yes. We're professionals. Of course my agent prefers we be more than that. It gives the media a lot to talk about. Are the kisses the real thing? And how far did we actually go in the love scenes? That sort of thing."

He wondered how she managed to live that way, having her business out there for everyone to see. But then, there were a number of politicians who lived the same way. He wasn't one of them and didn't plan to be. When he could get away from Washington, he usually did, by hightailing it back to Alaska.

"Do you still go dogsledding?" she asked.

Jess wondered how she knew he'd been into that. He didn't recall ever mentioning it to her. His expression must have given him away since she said, "Charm told me. I asked her about it when I saw a photo of you that time I visited her."

He'd heard about her visit. He'd been away in DC at the time. She had been filming in Vancouver and caught a flight to visit Charm in Fairbanks. From there she'd flown to visit Bailey and Walker on Kodiak Island.

"Yes, I still do go dogsledding, whenever I can. There's nothing else like it."

When she made a face, he chuckled and said, "Don't tell me you can't handle cold weather."

"After having spent most of my life in Wyoming and Denver, I have no choice, but when I think of doing something like bundling up to ride on a dogsled, it doesn't sound like anything I'd do."

"Hey, don't knock it until you try it. I have a feeling you just might like it."

"Why would you say that?" she asked.

"I say it because you come across as someone who isn't afraid to try something new and different, Paige."

He hoped like hell that was true, he thought as they entered the Windemere Resort. He was about to start throwing her all kinds of curveballs with the faith that one would eventually land right in her lap.

The notion that no one would recognize her vanished from Paige's mind the moment they walked into the restaurant and headed over to the counter to be seated. The hostess's eyes widened, and her mouth formed an O.

Before she could speak, Jess, who'd been standing by Paige's side, said, "Good morning. We would like a table for two in an area where we can see the lake, please."

The young woman, who looked to be in her early twenties, blinked again before giving Jess an astonished smile.

"Certainly, sir." Then she looked back at Paige. "You're Paige Novak, the actress, right?"

Paige smiled. "Yes." The woman might be looking at her, but she was also giving Jess the eye. Paige couldn't much blame her.

"I've seen all your movies and even watched you on that soap, *Touch the Heart.* Since they didn't kill you off, I'm hoping that means you might be coming back."

Paige's smile widened. "There's always that possibility."

The woman, whose name tag said Tobi, nodded and then glanced back over at Jess. He must have smiled at her because Tobi looked like she would melt in a puddle in front of them.

"Do you have any tables available?" Paige asked.

"Yes. Right this way."

They followed Tobi, and warmth raced through Paige when she felt Jess's palm at the center of her back. The restaurant was crowded, but she didn't have to look around to know that once again she'd been recognized. Soft murmurs flowed around them with a few gasps, and she could hear the clicking of cell phones letting her know photos of her and Jess were being taken.

Tobi led them to a table in the back next to a window. Jess pulled out the chair for her and suddenly she realized Kemp hadn't ever done anything so courteous. It hadn't bothered her because she could certainly pull out her own chair, but the gesture from Jess reminded her that with some men, especially those with Westmoreland blood flowing through their veins, manners were ingrained. Kemp, on the other hand, didn't have a chivalrous bone in his body.

"Your server will be here in a minute," Tobi said, handing them menus. Before walking off, she asked, "You've been here at the resort all this time?"

Paige had anticipated that question from someone today and gave her the response she, Jess, Spencer and Chardonnay had agreed on. "No, I'm on vacation visiting friends, Spencer and Chardonnay Westmoreland, at the Russell Vineyards."

Tobi blinked again. There was no doubt in Paige's mind that, as an employee of the resort, Tobi knew who owned the place. "The Westmorelands?"

"Yes."

Then, as if Tobi didn't want word to get back to the resort owner that she'd been taking up too much of Paige's time, she said, "Welcome to Windemere."

"Thank you."

When Tobi walked off, Paige glanced over at Jess and smiled. "So far, so good."

So far, so good was an understatement, Jess thought a short while later. Their server placed their breakfast plates in front of them, and he didn't need to look around to know photos were being taken. The clicking sound was all over the restaurant.

"Everything looks delicious, doesn't it?" she said, glancing up to find him staring at her. Hell, everyone snapping their photo would have captured him staring at her like a besotted fool. But then, that was a good thing. He wanted everyone to know just how taken he was with her. Truly.

He nodded. "Yes, everything does," he said, as he picked up his coffee cup, breaking eye contact.

She took a bite of bacon and gave him a dreamy smile. One he wished he could kiss right off her face, only to have it come back to kiss again. "The bacon is crisp, just the way I like it."

"Mine is cooked just the way I like it, too."

The couple sitting at the table next to theirs kept glancing over at them, and it was obvious the woman was trying to eavesdrop on their conversation.

"Did I tell you how beautiful you look this morning, Paige?"

"Yes, you did, and I'm looking forward to dining with you at Sedrick's tonight." There—she'd deliberately given the eavesdropping woman information that hopefully would be shared with the media.

"I'm glad we hooked up while on vacation," he said.

"So am I, Jess."

Not to be caught in lies unnecessarily, they had decided to be truthful about their relationship as much as possible. They would merely say that since the two of them were vacationing together with relatives and friends, they'd decided to spend time together. Their body language, facial expressions and physical responses would denote to any onlookers just how much and to what degree they enjoyed spending time together.

Jess figured that would be a piece of cake for him because every part of his body yearned for Paige. He wanted to touch her, taste her. More importantly, a part of him wanted to protect her from the Kemp Piersons of the world.

"When I talked to Pam last night, she mentioned that Crystal had delivered her triplets. Mom, babies and Daddy Bane are doing great," she said, breaking into his thoughts.

He nodded, smiling. "That's good to hear. More Westmorelands."

Jess and Paige then talked about the names Bane and Crystal had decided on for their sons. At least, she talked. He listened while watching her closely. He actually found the movement of her mouth fascinating. The same thing had happened last night when she'd been eating pizza. He'd never thought of a woman eating as erotic, but sharing a meal with Paige had definitely made him reach that conclusion.

"Other than dogsledding, what else do you like to do, Jess?"

He lifted his eyes to Paige and instantly his arousal shot up another notch. "I like playing cards."

"Oh? What do you play?"

"Mostly poker."

"A true Westmoreland. They all like playing poker. In fact, that's how it goes whenever they get together."

"I know. I've been part of their poker games before," he said, grinning.

"That's how I learned to play," she said. "Zane, Canyon and Jason taught me, but I'm far from being a card shark."

He was about to suggest they play a game of poker while they were here. Just the two of them. Hmm... strip poker would be nice.

"Anything else you like to do?" she asked.

He shrugged. "I like to dabble in paint every once in a while."

Her eyes widened in surprise. "You're an artist?"

"I wouldn't claim that, but I'm not so bad. It's a way for me to relax."

"Do you have anything that you've done that you're proud to display?"

"Display?" He chuckled. "No farther than my phone, trust me." He pulled out his phone from his back pocket. After clicking it on, he scrolled through several photos until he came to one particular picture. "I usually paint scenes and not people, but Dad commissioned me to do a painting of a person," he said, handing her the phone.

He watched her study the image. "You did a great job. She's beautiful. Who is she?"

"Claudia Dermotte, Charm's mother."

"She doesn't look old enough to have a daughter Charm's age."

"That's what most people say. She could be Charm's sister instead of her mother. She was only twenty-one when Charm was born, a lot younger than Bart. But then, most of his wives were. Claudia is the love of

Bart's life and the one woman who refused to marry him and the only one he can't control."

Jess and his brothers thought that was an understatement. Bart loved Claudia, and they figured she loved him, too, but she refused to put up with Bart's arrogant attitude. That was one reason he was always on good behavior around her. Um...maybe *good* was pushing it too much. *Acceptable* behavior was probably a better word.

"I'm surprised you haven't seen her before," Jess said.

Paige continued to study the image. "No, I've never seen or met Charm's mother. I didn't attend any Outlaw weddings due to being out of the country on film shoots, and I don't recall seeing her at Bailey and Walker's wedding."

"You wouldn't have. I'm sure you've heard that Bart is in denial as far as our relations to the Westmorelands are concerned. No one knows why. He's even approached a Westmoreland thinking it was his own son. That happened at Garth's rehearsal dinner—he tapped Riley on the shoulder thinking it was Garth. If anyone can find out why he feels that way, Claudia will be the one."

Paige glanced back at his cell phone. "Well, this is a beautiful painting and you're not giving yourself enough credit. You're truly gifted."

"One day I'd like to paint you, Paige," he said casually.

"You would?" she asked as her lips quirked in a smile.

"Yes."

"Then we're going to make sure that happens one of these days, Jess."

He nodded. Whether she knew it or not, he intended to make it happen.

Eight

"The Windemere Resort is amazing."

Paige looked at Jess, totally in agreement with what he said. "No matter how many times I come here, I can't get over how beautiful it is," she said as they walked the grounds. It was a gorgeous day, and although the sun was shining brightly, Napa Valley sat between two mountains that pretty much shielded the valley from the heat. That was also the reason for the cool nights.

"And I heard Spencer designed the resort himself," she added.

The moment they ended breakfast and left the restaurant and began walking around the resort, it was obvious that more people had recognized her. A text from Nadia just moments ago had informed them that Paige's appearance with a very handsome man was all over social media with pictures. Everyone was scrambling to determine Jess's identity.

Jess had a firm grip on her hand. They appeared as if they were any other normal couple spending time at the resort. More than once, Jess had touched the bare skin at the center of her back. He'd also brushed his thumb over her knuckles a few times and placed his arm around her shoulders. If she didn't know better, she would think he couldn't keep from touching her, but she knew he was just trying to display tenderness, affection and even possessiveness to anyone watching them. And there was no doubt in her mind they were being watched and filmed. People were whipping out their cameras left and right, although no one had approached them.

Paige glanced at her watch. They had been at the resort for four hours and it was time to head back to the vineyards if they wanted to rest up for dinner. By then, the media would be out in full force, and she and Jess needed to be ready.

"It's time to head back," she said.

"All right. What do you plan to do until dinner?"

She shrugged. "Take a nap, and then when I wake up I'll work on my hair."

He glanced at her head. "What's wrong with your hair?"

"I want to fix it differently tonight. I really want to look pretty."

He gave her a disbelieving look before saying, "You're always pretty, Paige. I think you're beautiful."

Appreciating the compliment, she reached up and

cupped his cheek, smiling at him. "That's a nice thing to say, Jess." At that very moment, a woman snapped a picture.

Grinning at her, Jess whispered, "I recall a time cell phones didn't come with cameras."

"The good old days?" Paige asked, chuckling.

"Yes, the good old days. I think our work for today is finished." As he still held tight to her hand, they walked toward the parking lot to leave.

Less than a half hour later, Paige was back at her villa and Jess was headed to the guest pool for a swim when her phone rang. It was Nadia.

"You again?"

Nadia laughed. "Sister-girl, you and Jess are blowing up the internet. The media did their research, and Jess has been identified. Pictures are all over the place of him as a dogsledder and he looks hot. They even found a calendar a few years ago that he did for some charity in Alaska where he was Mr. December, and trust me, December never looked so good. The women are going crazy."

Paige shook her head. "At least they don't think I went from a prince to a toad."

"Far from it. Some think he's hotter than Kemp. You should read their comments."

"I'll pass since you're reading them for me anyway."

"And I'm enjoying doing so. Right now the one with the most 'likes' is the one with your hand on his cheek. Dang it, Paige, that picture is so romantic. I could feel the chemistry between the two of you."

Paige rolled her eyes. "You could not."

"I could, too. You guys are laying it on thick."

Were they? Of course they wanted to come across as a couple who enjoyed being together. That way everyone could see Jess as someone who would make moving on easy.

And honestly, he was. She was comfortable with Jess. Conversation between them flowed easily. He'd told her about his dogsledding days and she'd told him how hard it had been to get a part in any movie because she was an unknown.

"Tonight, we're going to dinner. Since we dropped the name of the restaurant several times today, I expect the media will be there waiting."

"Are the two of you ready for that?"

"Yes." She liked Jess a lot and there was no doubt everyone would be able to see it. Everyone other than Jess himself.

"I need to take a nap before getting ready."

"You and your naps. Okay, I'll keep you updated about what's happening on social media."

After ending the call with Nadia, Paige couldn't help checking to see any pictures. The first one she saw was the one where her hand was on Jess's cheek as they stared at each other. Nadia was right. It did look romantic. Just seeing the way he was looking at her had heat churning in her stomach. He had definitely gotten into the role of a man who desired a woman. She could see it in his eyes.

She then studied her own eyes and saw how intense they were as she looked at him. She didn't just look like a woman who desired a man, but a woman who was falling in love.

Paige blinked, knowing that just wasn't true, and figured that she was more tired than she'd thought. Her brain was turning to mush. She definitely needed a nap. She came to another "liked" photo and threw her hand over her mouth to stop screaming out in laughter. Someone had taken a photo, a pretty darn good one, of Jess's denim-clad ass. The post said, "I've never seen anything so yummy. Have you?"

Her phone suddenly rang, and she saw it was a call from Maxie. She took a deep breath, knowing her agent was probably not happy with her.

She clicked on. "Yes, Maxie?"

"I hope you know you've ruined your chances of ever getting another decent part in any movie production. Kemp Pierson is the hottest thing in Hollywood and it's unfortunate you couldn't appreciate that fact."

Paige frowned, fed up with Maxie's attitude. "What I couldn't appreciate is him messing around with Maya and thinking I'd forgive him, like it was nothing. What's even more disappointing is that you think I should go back to him for the sake of my career, Maxie."

"Some women have done worse, Paige. This is Hollywood. Kemp holds the title of Hottest Man Alive, and you were the woman by his side. People expect him to act indecent once in a while, and they expect you to get over it."

Paige's frown deepened. If she didn't know any better, she would think Kemp's affair with Maya had been part of some script for publicity. Had it? "Maybe that's the problem. If that's what people truly expect, well, I have news for them. I have moved on and I really like the guy I'm with now. He's kind and—"

"He's not Kemp Pierson."

"Thank God for that. Goodbye, Maxie."

Paige ended the call, then threw her head back to draw in a deep breath. Maxie had been her agent for five years and her contract was up for renewal. Maybe it was time to end things if the woman felt it was okay for Paige to lower her standards just because of Kemp's popularity. But then, she had a feeling she wouldn't have to bother. Maxie would probably be dropping her.

Just like she'd told Jill, she was prepared for the consequences.

Jess glanced at his watch as he made his way down the path to Paige's door. Hopefully, she wouldn't mind that he was a few minutes early. Adrenaline was flowing through his veins and it couldn't be helped. He wanted to see her again. He *needed* to see her again.

Upon returning to the villa after breakfast, he had changed clothes and gone swimming to work off his sexual frustration. He doubted Paige realized just what being around her had done to his libido. Spending most of the morning with her had reminded him that he still had one.

Since becoming a senator, he'd never lost sight of the reason he'd been sent to Washington, and he'd kept himself busy. He had dated a few women, but he knew he would not get serious about any of them. Whenever he'd needed a date to an event, Charm would fly in, and he'd been satisfied with that arrangement. No wonder his constituents had suggested he get a social life. And now, after spending the last couple of days with Paige, he would have to agree with them.

Jess knocked on the door, and it didn't take long for Paige to answer it. The moment he saw her he was glad his legs were planted firmly on the ground, otherwise he might have dropped to his knees. She was that gorgeous.

"Come in. I just need to grab my purse."

He entered, and by the time he could breathe again, she was back.

"How do I look?" she said, twirling around. Just like this morning, he noticed everything about her outfit. How the dress stopped above the knee...way above the knee...and fit her body, every single delectable curve, like it was hand painted on her. He was tempted to reach out and touch it to make sure it wasn't.

And then her hair... When she had twirled around, it had moved as if in slow motion, the waves fanning around her face. Knowing she was waiting for his response, he finally said, "You look magnificent, gorgeous, beautiful, stun—"

She threw up her hand and laughed. "No need to get carried away, Jess."

Was that what she thought? He was getting carried away? If she did, then she hadn't seen anything yet. And the sad thing was that this was not a ruse to him. This was the real thing, and he was as serious as he could get.

"I will say, Jess Outlaw, that you look rather dashing yourself. I love a man who wears a suit well, and trust me, you look good."

"Thanks. Luckily, I brought one with me for the anniversary party."

"Have you seen the comments being made about us on social media? Namely the ones about you?" she asked.

"No, but my brothers and Charm have. They called to tease me."

"Having regrets?"

He saw the concern in her features and shook his head. "Not a single one. My siblings wouldn't be who they are if they didn't rag me about anything. They know I'll take it in stride. In fact, Maverick told me to tell you that he would have loved to have flown here to be your love interest. He thinks I'm nothing but a stuffed shirt."

She leaned close and said, "I'd rather be with you than Maverick. He would have dumped me the second a woman with big boobs caught his eye."

Jess laughed. Although that did sound like something his baby brother would do, he couldn't imagine anyone dumping her. Even Kemp wasn't dumping her; he just wanted to have his cake and eat it, too.

"Is there anything we need to go over beforehand? The media can be fierce."

"I'm good. I've dealt with them before. My campaign in Alaska was anything but smooth." Jess offered her his arm. "Are you ready to go?"

She smiled at him and took it. "Yes, I'm ready."

Nine

Sedrick's was situated on a grassy slope in the heart of Napa Valley. The huge European-style structure was built of stone and brick and seemed to stand like an elite beacon. Lights surrounded the establishment and Paige noted most of the cars in the parking lot were expensive, which pretty much defined the restaurant's clientele. This was a Thursday night, and if the full parking lot was anything to go by, the place was packed.

Jess had told her on the drive over that he'd made reservations and would be using Spencer and Chardonnay's private room. On their first date, Spencer had brought Chardonnay here, and eventually he'd struck a deal with the owner to have that private room always available for whenever he and Chardonnay returned here to dine. Paige had never heard of anyone owning a room in a restaurant, but somehow Spencer, being the astute businessman that he was, had become a silent partner with that benefit.

She glanced over at Jess and recalled the moment she'd opened her door for him. His gaze had roamed her from head to toe, and she'd sworn she'd seen deep male appreciation in his eyes. Desire was something most men couldn't hide. Seeing that look had sent heat rolling around in her stomach, and she had even felt the tips of her nipples harden against the fabric of her dress. She had to remind herself she had recognized desire in his eyes six years ago, too, but he hadn't acted on it then, and chances were, he wouldn't do so now.

A valet quickly moved forward to greet them and his smile widened when he saw her. Opening her car door, he said, "Welcome to Sedrick's, Miss Novak."

"Thank you."

Jess came around the car to stand by her side as he handed the attendant the keys. No sooner had they rounded the corner to the restaurant's entrance than reporters appeared, swarming around them with their cameras flashing.

"Is it true you've been hiding out here in Napa Valley all this time, Miss Novak?" a reporter asked as flash-bulbs fired off in her and Jess's faces. The feel of his hand at the center of her back gave her comfort.

She smiled at the reporter. "Hiding out? That's definitely not true. As you know, I just finished filming in Japan and decided to take a vacation and visit my cousins-in-law, the Westmorelands, at Russell Vineyards for a bit of rest and relaxation."

"And why weren't you available to make a statement?" another reporter asked.

Paige smiled. "There was nothing for me to say. I'd spoken with Kemp. He knows I've moved on and I wish him the best."

"So, the two of you are no longer together?"

She was about to reiterate when Jess surprised her by saying, "As Paige stated, she has moved on, and I'm more than happy to help her do so."

With Jess's statement, the reporters' attention was now on him. "Senator Outlaw, are you and Miss Novak involved in a 'hot, romantic entanglement' as her sister claims? And if so, does it not bother you that Miss Novak jumped into a relationship with you so soon after ending one with Kemp Pierson?"

Jess chuckled. "I refuse to comment on the first question, and as far as the second question goes, the answer is no. The timing of Paige's breakup with Pierson doesn't bother me. In fact, I feel that now is the perfect time for me to do what I didn't do a few years ago when I first met Paige."

"And what was that?" a couple of reporters asked at once.

"Make sure she knows just how taken I am with her," Jess said. Paige stood beside him and smiled, thinking the reporters were eating up the fake story Jess was weaving.

"And why didn't you make your move then?" a female reporter asked.

"At the time, I was knee-deep in my campaign and was only focused on that. I've run into Paige over the years, but she was either filming or I was getting settled in Washington as a senator. When I was finally ready to make my move, she had become involved with someone."

Paige noted Jess refused to mention Kemp by name. He paused. "All that is behind us, and this is the perfect time for me and Paige to enjoy each other's company without any distractions."

"What about the comment Kemp Pierson made about the two of you still being together, Miss Novak?"

Paige eased closer to Jess's side, and he slid what appeared to be a possessive arm around her waist. "As I've stated, Kemp and I are *not* together, and he knows that. As you can see, I'm here with Jess, and there's no other person I'd rather spend my vacation with."

She glanced up at Jess and noted the intense way he was staring at her. A very sensuous look. Suddenly, it was as if all the reporters faded to the background, and Jess began lowering his head to hers.

He was going to kiss her.

They hadn't discussed the possibility of sharing a kiss, but it would make sense, to substantiate all they'd said tonight. She turned into Jess's arms, and when his mouth connected to hers, she ignored the multitude of bulbs flashing to capture their kiss. If ever there was a kiss designed to render a person senseless, this one was it.

This wasn't a regular kiss—it was hungry, seductive and possessive—and she returned it in kind, not caring about the photographers or reporters or those dining in the restaurant who could probably see them. Nothing mattered to Paige but this, the feel of Jess's lips on hers and the taste of his tongue in her mouth.

Although they had given the reporters more than enough coverage tonight, Paige wasn't ready to end the kiss and would still be in Jess's arms if one of the reporters hadn't said, "Kemp Pierson is going to blow a fuse when he sees that Paige has moved on."

"But then, what did he expect after being unfaithful to her?" another reporter asked.

Paige drew her mouth away from Jess. If he kissed like this with an audience, how would he kiss in private? Tasting him on her lips, she turned to the reporters. Before she could say anything, one asked, "What about what the senator said? Will you let him show you how taken he is with you?"

Paige chuckled. "Most definitely."

"And what do the two of you anticipate happening while vacationing here in Napa Valley?"

Paige glanced up at Jess and smiled sweetly before saying, "You know the saying—what happens on vacation…"

She left the sentence hanging, and Paige thought that was a perfect way to end their time with the reporters. "Jess and I will be going inside to enjoy our dinner. Good night, everyone."

With his arm still placed possessively around her waist, Jess escorted her into the restaurant.

Jess kept his hand at the center of Paige's back as the maître d' escorted them through the mass of well-dressed patrons. A number stared at them with huge grins on their faces. There was no doubt in his mind some had probably witnessed his and Paige's first kiss. Granted, he wished it hadn't been done to put on a show. Even so, he still got the Paige-effect from mingling his tongue with hers, and parts of his body were still raging with need for another kiss. The next one would be private and just as potent.

They continued following the maître d' until they reached a private room in the back. The man opened the door to a space with brick walls, dark wooden beams, cast-iron chandeliers and a beautiful table set for two. The size of the room was no larger than one's dining room, but the entire area held an ambience of romance.

After being seated and given menus and the wine list, they were told that only wine from the Russell Vineyards could be served in this room. The maître d' then informed them their waitress would arrive soon to take their dinner order and wine selection.

The second they were alone, Paige smiled and said, "I think the interview with those reporters went great. You're the one who should be the actor, Jess. What you said sounded so believable, and I can't wait to see how those reporters will spin things."

He returned her smile. Eventually she would figure out nothing had been playacting on his part. What he'd told those reporters had been the truth. He figured he had caught her off guard with that kiss and his possessiveness, but he had been acting on male instincts and nothing more. A lot could happen on vacation and he intended to make sure theirs was one neither of them would forget.

They studied their menus and wine list and agreed on what they would have. The door opened and a waitress came in and they gave the woman their order. She was back within minutes to pour their wine and leave a basket of bread on the table.

"I like this room," he said, once they were alone again. "I see why it has sentimental significance for Spencer and Chardonnay."

She nodded. "It is nice, and the view from that window is awesome." Buttering one of the breads from the basket, she asked, "Is there any place that has sentimental significance for you?"

That one was easy. "Yes, in fact, there is such a place," he said.

"Where?"

"The Westmoreland House that Dillon built on his property."

She smiled at his mention of a place so special to her family. "When Pam and Dillon married, it was important for his family to know she wasn't taking him away from them, that they would always remain a big part of the family, so she implemented a huge dinner in their home once a month and all the family was invited. At the time, Dillon was the only one who was married."

She took another sip of her wine, and from her expression, Jess could tell she liked it. "Anyway," she continued, "the once-a-month dinners became twice-a-month dinners when more Westmoreland men got married and everyone began having children. Dillon has a huge house, but pretty soon the dining room couldn't accommodate everyone, so he and Pam came up with the idea to build the Westmoreland House on his property. It has a humongous kitchen, where all the wives can help with the cooking, and a dining area that seats over two hundred. It's plenty big enough when the Atlanta, Montana and Texas Westmorelands come to visit. And now the Outlaws. Of course, the men insisted the Westmoreland House have a man cave where they can play poker. Which made the women insist on having a theater room to watch movies. And they even added a game room for the teens and a playroom for the little ones. Everyone is happy."

After biting into her bread, Paige asked, "Why would the Westmoreland House be of any sentimental significance to you, Jess?"

He took a sip of his own wine before saying, "Because it was there, where Pam and Dillon hosted that holiday dinner and invited the Outlaws, that I saw you for the first time."

Paige tilted her head and gazed at Jess. Why would he say such a thing now when no reporters were around? They were alone. And why was he looking at her like that over the rim of his wineglass? Perhaps they'd taken their playacting a little too far... He had to have been joking, although he looked serious. A part of her refused to go there.

"Did you know Russell will start taking classes at the Napa Valley Wine Academy this fall?"

In a way, Paige was grateful for the transition in conversation. "While in high school?"

"Yes. It's part of a dual enrollment program. He's decided to follow his father into finance. But unlike Spencer, who got his MBA from the University of Southern California, Russell wants to be a Harvard man."

"Well, I can certainly see him working by his father's side as he gets older. More than once, Spencer has stated he's building his empire to pass on to his children."

Then they began discussing various other subjects and he mentioned that his cousin Delaney and her husband, Jamal, had issued a personal invitation to the Outlaws to visit them in the Middle East.

"Do you plan to go?" she asked him.

"I'm thinking about it. Reggie, Olivia and their kids are there now. I understand Reggie and Delaney were besties while growing up."

She nodded. Senator Reginald Westmoreland, or Reggie, as everyone called him, was one of Jess's Westmoreland cousins. "Yes, that's what I heard as well." Was she imagining things or was Jess staring at her mouth? Did he find her lips as fascinating as she found his?

"Paige?"

She blinked and shifted her gaze from his mouth to his eyes. "Yes?"

"I was asking you a question."

Oops. "Sorry, my mind was elsewhere. Could you repeat it?"

"Sure. I asked if I could paint a portrait of you while you're here."

Paige couldn't imagine sitting before him, quiet and unmoving, staring at him without drooling. Luckily, she was spared from giving Jess an answer when the waitress arrived with their food.

Ten

Paige still hadn't given him an answer to his question, Jess thought, when he brought the car to a stop in front of the main house at Russell Vineyards. Over dinner she had kept the conversation lively, but hadn't gone back to him painting her. Why?

There hadn't been any reporters waiting on them when they'd left the restaurant. Evidently, they had given the media enough information before going inside. He could just imagine the stories that would appear when they logged on later.

"Thank you for such a lovely evening, Jess."

"You're welcome. It's still early yet. How about us killing that last bottle of wine from the other night?" He figured they could handle it since they'd only had a glass at dinner. They had ordered coffee with their dessert.

Jess couldn't help getting turned on whenever Paige began nibbling on her lips, like she was doing now. They were lips he wanted to taste again. "And you never gave me an answer to my question about painting you."

"I wouldn't want you to go to any trouble."

"No trouble at all. Like I told you earlier today, I prefer painting scenery, but you will be a beautiful subject with the vineyards as the backdrop. In fact, I saw the perfect spot while out jogging this morning."

"You did?"

"Yes. The moment I saw it, I knew I had to paint you there. It would be a great addition for my home in DC."

He saw her brow lift. "You would hang it in your home?"

"Of course. Then whenever I look at it, I will have memories of my time with you."

"Oh."

She began nibbling her bottom lip, a gesture he'd come to realize meant she was thinking hard. Good. He added, "I've enjoyed spending time with you these past couple of days, getting to know you, Paige. Over the next weeks, I hope to get to know even more about you."

She glanced over at him. "I've enjoyed spending time with you as well, and look forward to getting to know you better," she said softly. "But…"

He studied her features. "But what?"

She looked away, tracing the edge of the leather seat with her fingertips. When she didn't say anything and refused to look at him, he gently caught her wrist in his hand. When she glanced up at him, the look he saw in her eyes made his heart ache. "Tell me, Paige. But what?"

"But I'm not sure where all this will end or what you expect of our time together, Jess. There is chemistry between us and it's strong. I can feel it. At first, I thought it was one-sided, but I'm not sure that it is."

Jess decided to be honest with her. "It's not one-sided. I can feel it as well. But then, I think that's understandable. You are a very beautiful woman."

"Thank you, and you're a very handsome man. However, I feel as if my life is pretty messy right now."

He could understand her still having feelings for Kemp, no matter what he'd done. When you loved someone and they betrayed you, you hurt, but the love didn't go away immediately. He understood that. It had taken him a while to get over Ava, but he had gotten over her. The same would happen with Paige…with the right person in her life.

"Since we need to spend time together for the media, Paige, then let me help you get your life un-messy," he said, tucking a strand of hair behind her ear. "All I want is to help you get through a rough time, Paige. I'm honestly not expecting anything."

That wasn't totally true. What he did expect was to leave an impression on her. A positive impression, and just like he'd told Garth, hopefully, when she was ready to move on and indulge in a serious relationship, she would recall that he was a pretty likable guy, a man who would appreciate the woman she was. Over the course of the following weeks, he was going to do whatever it took to make sure of it.

She nodded. "Okay."

He raised a questioning brow. "Okay what?"

"I could definitely enjoy having my life un-rattled, Jess."

He tilted his head and looked at her. "When was the last time you had some real honest-to-goodness fun, Paige?"

The fact that she had to think hard about his question let him know it had been too long.

"I honestly can't remember," she murmured softly.

"Then let's make this a fun vacation."

A slow smile touched her lips. "I'd like that, and since I'm not a good planner of fun stuff, I'll leave it up to you."

He was not sure that was such a good idea when even now he loved the scent of her and wanted to breathe her all in. A part of him wanted to pull her into his lap to taste her lips again. He doubted she had any idea just how much he wanted her. How much he intended to leave an impression on her, both mentally and physically.

"I have no problem doing that," he said, still holding her wrist and loving the feel of her skin in his hand. "So, what about that third bottle of wine?"

"Wine sounds great. And, Jess?"

"Yes?"

"I'm not that twenty-two-year-old girl anymore," she said.

He released a gusty breath. Was there a specific reason she was telling him that? He could definitely see that she had matured into an even more gorgeous woman. "And I will enjoy getting to know the older woman you've become, Paige."

* * *

It was a nice night, although being smack in the middle of two mountains made the temperature cool. However, as they walked toward Jess's villa, the cool air wasn't the main thing on Paige's mind. He was.

Although she had told him that she wasn't ready for a serious relationship, she had no qualms about indulging in a nonserious one. She definitely didn't have a problem enjoying her time with him. She wondered how Jess would react if he knew the one thing that had remained constant over the years was that he was still her fantasy man.

And what if, while getting to know each other, all that sexual chemistry got out of hand? Was a vacation fling—if it came to that—so bad? She couldn't forget that the only reason he was spending time with her was to help her out with the media. At the end of the month, he would go back to DC and she would return to Hollywood.

Six years ago, she'd been fresh out of college and ready to take on the world. She knew, without a doubt, that even if Jess had responded to all that flirting that she'd done, it would only have resulted in an affair. She would not have wanted anything more than that.

Did she want anything more now? She drew in a deep breath, knowing she wasn't sure. What she did know was that she would love more kisses like the one Jess had laid on her earlier tonight—the one that made her nipples hard just remembering it. With Kemp, she'd never come close to feeling the heat that one kiss with Jess had caused.

And then there was his touch. He'd slid his hand in hers the moment she'd gotten out of the car, and he was still holding it as they walked the path leading to his villa. She was amazed how easy it was for her body to react to him. How deep her attraction went. She could just imagine getting naked and being naughty with him. That kind of thought was territory she'd never moved into with another man, but she could definitely see going there with Jess. There was something about him that made her think things, want things and need things... How was that possible?

"You've gotten quiet, Paige."

She glanced over at him. "I was just thinking."

"About what?"

No way she would tell him what her true thoughts had been, so she said, "I was wondering if I should be concerned with what you might put on that 'fun' list. I guess now is a good time to let you know I'm not into mountain climbing."

He chuckled and the sound stirred something within her. "You're not?"

"No. Bailey tried teaching me and gave up."

Jess nodded. "Okay, then maybe you need to tell me some things we could do that might interest you," he said. "At breakfast you mentioned that you like horseback riding and skiing. There's no snow here, so skiing won't make the list."

"Phooey."

She heard his chuckle. It was rich and sexy. Just like the man himself. She was tempted to say he could add anything involving his mouth, tongue and hands to the list.

"Hopefully we'll come up with a few more things over wine."

"That sounds good to me." She glanced over at him. "So, when do you want to paint me?" Now that he had suggested it, she rather liked the idea.

"I'll be glad to show you the exact spot I have in mind tomorrow. I suggest we go jogging together. Afterward, we can go somewhere for breakfast and then make a stop to purchase paint supplies."

She liked that he was planning her into his day. "I'd like that."

"Here we are," he said, upon reaching his villa. After opening the door, he flipped on a light and then stood back to let her enter.

"Thanks," she said, walking to the living room. "I need to get out of these," she added, kicking off her three-inch heels.

"Your feet hurt?"

"They always do with new shoes that I haven't quite broken in." She glanced around and then asked, "Are we doing it in the living room or the kitchen?" Too late she realized how that sounded and quickly said, "What I meant was—"

"I know what you meant," he said, removing his dinner jacket to hang it neatly on the coat tree while flashing that dimple in his chin when his lips began twitching.

Paige hoped he never stopped doing that. Smiling at her. Showing that dimple.

"I prefer the living room, if that's okay," Jess said in a husky voice.

"That's fine with me," she said, trying not to blush. "If you want to grab the glasses from the cabinet, then I'll grab the wine."

Heaven help me, Jess thought, loosening his tie while following Paige into the kitchen.

Those legs, bare feet or in heels, were such a gorgeous pair in that damn sexy dress on such a delectable little body—she was almost giving him heart failure. And then there was that ass. He had no choice but to look when he had to walk around the island to grab the wineglasses out of the cabinet. He had intended to take things slow with Paige, but damn, she made him want to speed things up a bit.

"Ready?" she asked, after he rinsed out the glasses. He hadn't known she was still there. He'd assumed she had grabbed the wine bottle and headed to the living room.

"Yes," he said, moving around the island to walk beside her to the other room.

He watched as Paige placed the wine on the coffee table, before sitting down on the sofa and tucking her legs beneath her. He exhaled deeply, trying to recall the last time he'd been faced with such temptation. Of course she would choose that moment to look at him, raise a questioning brow and ask, "What's wrong?"

Too late. He'd been caught staring. "Nothing. I was just thinking about something." He poured their wine, and then, fighting for control, he took a sip. "You want to tell me some of the things you'd like for us to do together for fun, Paige?"

She took a sip of her own wine and said, "Other than the mountain climbing thing, I'm open to just about anything."

He nodded, wondering if she knew what "just about anything" could entail in his book. "What about riding in a hot-air balloon over the valley?"

Paige giggled and he loved the sound of her laugh. "I've never done that before, but it sounds like fun. Please add it to the list."

"What about bike riding?"

"Wow," she said, brushing her hair back from her face. "I haven't done that in years. I'd love to. And don't forget horseback riding. And swimming. I love swimming."

Jess smiled. "Okay, we have a few things on the list. We'll start with those."

"Sounds good to me."

"And I figure if we spend a couple of hours each day painting, preferably in the evenings, I should be able to finish in a week or less."

"That soon?" she asked, shifting positions on the sofa to untuck her legs. Jess watched as she smoothed her hand down one leg and then the other, kneading the muscles there.

"Are you okay?" he asked.

"Yes, I'm fine. My legs got a cramp. It happens sometimes when I sit in that position too long."

"Maybe I can help," he said, crossing the room to sit on the sofa. "Scoot sideways," he said. After she followed his instructions, he reached out and pulled her legs into his lap.

"I'll massage the cramp away," he said, gently rubbing the palm of his hand into the muscles of her legs and then slowly moving downward toward her feet. He hadn't seen her coral nail polish before now. He liked it.

"That feels good," she said softly. She had closed her eyes.

"I'm glad you're enjoying it."

"I've enjoyed everything about tonight, Jess."

That was good to hear, he thought, because he'd enjoyed everything about tonight as well. He especially liked this, massaging inch after inch of one leg and then the other, the feel of her satiny smooth skin.

Jess trailed his gaze upward to her face and studied her features. With her eyes closed she looked peaceful. Not for the first time, he wondered how any man could be unfaithful to such a gorgeous creature. "You okay?" he asked huskily.

"Yes," she responded, curving her lips in a smile, without opening her eyes. "Your hands feel nice, Jess."

His gaze moved from her face downward to her chest. Her arms were folded under her breasts, lifting them provocatively against the neckline of her dress. He licked his lips and imagined skimming the nipples with his fingertips before taking them into his mouth. Feeling his control slipping, and knowing his lusty thoughts would only get him in trouble, he returned his gaze to her face.

Her eyes were open, and she was staring at him. There was no way she hadn't noticed the attention he'd given her breasts. And she'd probably seen when he'd licked his lips while looking at them. Their gazes held for a long moment, and sexual chemistry flowed between them, sucking them in. There was no way she couldn't feel his erection growing beneath her leg.

She finally broke the silence, and with her eyes still glued to his, she whispered, "Do you know what else I enjoyed about tonight, Jess?" Her voice was so soft that it stroked his insides. All the way to his groin.

"No, Paige, what else did you enjoy about tonight?" he asked, not caring if she saw the intense heat in his gaze.

"Our kiss."

Damn. He could recall the way her lips had fit to his, how easy it had been for his tongue to slide into her mouth, wrap around hers. He could even recall the breathy moan she'd made when he had deepened the hottest kiss he'd ever shared with a woman. Neither he nor Paige had cared that they'd had an audience.

Now they were in his villa. Alone.

More than anything, he wanted to feast on her mouth. Her eyes were pinned to his, and he felt a need so intense, it made him intoxicated. Not able to resist any longer, he pulled her into his arms and covered her mouth with his.

Eleven

The moment Paige knew the kiss was coming, she opened her mouth so Jess's tongue could easily slide inside. Even with an audience, his mouth had held nothing back. It had taken hers, making every cell in her body respond to the way their tongues had tangled.

With this kiss, he was taking it up a notch—maybe two.

Suddenly, he broke off the kiss and rested his forehead against hers as they both breathed in. Moments later, he leaned back and stared at her. Chemistry floated all around them, making the air crackle and pop with sexual energy. She felt it and wanted nothing more than to rejoin their mouths again in deep, heated bliss.

"I need to get you home, Paige," he finally said.

She blinked. Did he just say he needed to get her

home and not that he intended to sweep her into his arms and head for his bedroom? She tilted her head and could see desire in his eyes the way she knew it was in hers. Even now, anticipation thickened the air, so what was going on?

As if he knew her thoughts, he said, "When we make love, I want you to be ready, and I don't want to rush things with you, Paige."

Holy crap. He didn't want to rush things? He couldn't rush a woman whose body felt like a massive sensual throb. A woman who needed sexual relief. And as far as readiness went, the buildup had started the moment he'd arrived on her doorstep for dinner. Just seeing him at the door had stirred something within her. Then later that kiss had ignited the fire. Being in his presence, sitting across from him at dinner, seeing his smile and hearing his sexy voice had kept the fire roaring. Then his touch on her legs, followed by their second kiss, had set the fire ablaze. Now he wanted to put it out?

"The last thing I want to do is to come across as a sex-crazed guy, Paige," he said, his words intruding into her thoughts.

She nibbled on her bottom lip. If he had any idea how long it had been since the last time she'd had sex, he would know *sex-crazed* sounded pretty darn good to her right now. Before she could respond, he eased her legs off his lap to stand. Shoving his hand into his pocket, he said, "I doubt you know how hard this is for me."

If his erection was anything to go by, yes, it obviously was hard. Literally. "You don't think I'm ready for you?" Even now, he'd made her panties wet.

"I want you ready both physically and mentally. I admit that in my younger days I was into one-nighters and wham-bam-thank-you-ma'am sex, but not now and definitely not with you."

She frowned. Why was he making this such a big deal? She wasn't asking for a ring on her finger or a declaration of undying love. "I'm not looking for anything serious," she said, in case he assumed that.

"I know you aren't, and you shouldn't this soon anyway. I won't take advantage of your vulnerability."

Paige squared her shoulders. "How noble. And this nobility will last how long, exactly?" she asked, trying to keep the disappointment out of her voice.

"Not sure. I haven't been with a woman in almost a year, Paige. As a result, my sexual hunger is at an all-time high. You are a very desirable woman who has filled my mind with lusty thoughts. However, when it comes to you, I refuse to think with the wrong head."

He hadn't been with a woman in almost a year? With his looks, there was no way women hadn't come on to him. So why had he denied himself sexual pleasure?

As if he read the question in her eyes, he said, "I haven't had the time."

It had been six months for her. No wonder they were like a spontaneous combustion. The very idea relit her fire.

Standing, she eased close to him and wrapped her arms around his neck. Before she could open her mouth to comment, he said, "Don't tempt me, Paige. I've made my decision about tonight. You need to sleep on what I said, and if tomorrow you're ready to take me on, just let me know."

And then he swept her into his arms.

"We'll grab your shoes on the way out. I'm taking you home."

He was actually taking her home. "I can walk, Jess."

"I'd rather carry you there." He didn't say anything for a moment, and then he added, "Be forewarned, Paige. Once I'm certain that you're ready to take me on, our 'hot, romantic entanglement' will begin, and I won't hold anything back."

Not to be outdone, she said, "And be forewarned, Jess. I don't plan to hold anything back either."

Jess needed a drink. He'd just returned from carrying Paige home, literally, and now he was trying to convince himself he had done the right thing by waiting. Even now, he was tempted to walk back down the path, knock on her door and tell her he'd changed his mind. However, what held him back was knowing his actions tonight were part of his strategic planning.

She might not think one night would make all the difference in the world, but it did. He needed to show her that she meant more to him than being a one-night stand. Hell, she was more than a casual fling, but she'd have to realize that for herself. Of course, with a little help from him.

Like before, whenever she came and left, her scent lingered. At her door he'd told her to get a good night's sleep. Now chances were, he wouldn't. He glanced at their wineglasses that had been left on the coffee table. The wine bottle was half-full. Instead of drinking and talking, they'd been kissing. He wouldn't complain about that.

Now he needed a drink, but something stronger than wine. Spencer had mentioned he'd put a bottle of cognac, Jess's drink of choice, in the cabinet over the refrigerator. He appreciated his cousin for doing so because tonight he definitely needed it. He left the wine bottle on the coffee table with hopes he and Paige would eventually finish it. Grabbing their glasses, he then took them to the kitchen to rinse out and place in the dishwasher.

He found the bottle of cognac just where Spencer said it would be, and after grabbing a glass, he headed to the patio. Tonight, he needed to sit, drink, plan and strategize.

Dinner had been delicious and intimate. That private room had been perfect, and sitting across from Paige, seeing how her beautiful features had reflected in the moonlight and listening to her hold a conversation with both intelligence and insight had been enlightening. She might travel the globe a lot, but she kept up with the national news. All of their conversations during dinner had been interesting.

Jess glanced over at the villa where Paige was staying. A couple of her lights were still on; he'd flipped all his out. He much preferred the darkness, the peace and quiet. He'd taken a few sips of cognac before leaning back in the chair to close his eyes. It had been a long day, but a productive one. He hoped like hell that Kemp Pierson had egg all over his face tomorrow.

He opened his eyes when he heard a sound. Straining to see in the dark, he could make out Paige in the moonlight and in the lights lining the path. He sat up straight in his chair. Where in the hell was she going? It was past midnight. He studied her attire, saw the bathing robe and then figured she was going for a swim. At this hour? Why wasn't she in bed?

Why aren't you? he asked himself as he watched her stroll up the path. She didn't even glance over at his place, probably figuring, since all the lights were out in his villa, that he'd gone to bed. Although he knew Russell Vineyards was pretty safe twenty-four hours a day, and the pool was well lit, he still didn't like the idea of her going there alone. What if she slipped and bumped her head? What if she got another cramp in her legs while swimming? What if…?

Jess rubbed his hand down his face. What if he stopped coming up with these crazy scenarios that likely wouldn't happen? When Paige took a turn and was no longer within his sight, he stood, deciding he would check on her to make sure she was okay. There was no way he could sleep until he knew for certain she was fine.

Paige glided through the Olympic-size pool, doing laps. The water was warm and wonderful over her skin. Tonight, she had felt undeniably hot for Jess, to the point where she'd decided to go swimming to cool off and work off sexual frustrations.

"…I haven't been with a woman in almost a year, Paige. As a result, my sexual hunger is at an all-time high…"

Jess's words kept flowing through her mind as she

stroked her way through the water. *Almost a year?* He definitely had to be ready for sex, yet he'd refused to make love to her until he was certain she was ready to take him on. She couldn't wait until she saw him tomorrow. She'd show him what readiness looked like.

Paige continued swimming, thinking about the articles about her and Jess that would hit in the morning. Kemp and Maxie would be pissed, but she didn't care. How Kemp dealt with the true status of their relationship was his problem, not hers.

Jess was her problem.

She had wanted him tonight more than she'd ever wanted a man before. He had stroked something within her that she hadn't known was there. Real passion. She would listen to Jill tell her and Nadia just how wonderful making love was, and Paige had known she'd been missing out on something. Nadia hadn't contributed to the conversation one way or the other since she thought no man alive was worth sharing her bed until she got good and ready, and she wasn't ready.

Paige, on the other hand, had had her first sexual encounter in college. Alvin Lanford had been such a big disappointment, and so had the next guy, Marion Bovina. She had decided she'd had it with the bedroom until Kemp. She'd expected him to rock her world. Um, not at all. She had begun thinking that maybe the problem was her and not her bed partners.

However, she would have to say, neither Alvin, Marion or Kemp had turned her on with a mere kiss the way Jess had. If he'd continued kissing her, she would have climaxed right then and there. Every part of her had felt alive, rejuvenated in a way that tingled. And for her that wasn't normal.

The only other time she had reacted that way to a man had been six years ago, and that man had been Jess. He hadn't touched her, hadn't even kissed her then, but her entire being had reacted the moment he had walked into the Westmoreland House. The moment their gazes had connected, she had felt a throbbing heat from the top of her head to the bottoms of her feet.

She swam back and forth doing more laps, trying to push everything and everyone from her mind. She wasn't sure how much longer she swam or how much longer she planned to keep swimming. It was getting late and Jess had put a lot on their agenda for tomorrow. She needed to get out and go to bed. Maybe now she would be able to sleep.

She swam to the pool's edge and got out of the water. Using the towel she'd brought with her, she began drying off. Suddenly, she heard a sound. Jerking around, she was surprised to see Jess.

Drawing in a deep breath from the fright he'd given her, she asked, "Jess, what are you doing here? Why aren't you in bed?"

"I could ask you the same thing, Paige," he said, coming closer to stand right in front of her. He was wearing the same clothes—dark slacks, white shirt but minus the tie. And from the look of things, his erection was making itself known. There were some things a man couldn't hide.

"I couldn't sleep," she finally said.

"Neither could I. I was sitting out on my patio when

I saw you leave the villa. I could tell by your outfit this was where you were headed."

She tilted her head to look up at him. "So, you followed me."

"Yes. I wanted to make sure you were okay."

She had been okay until she'd seen him just now. With him standing in front of her, all those sexual frustrations she had swum away were back in full force. "You didn't have to follow me. I felt safe coming here alone." Then she recalled what he'd said and asked, "You've been here the entire time? Watching me swim?" If that was true, no wonder he was aroused. Her skimpy two-piece bathing suit left little to the imagination. She might as well be swimming in a bra and thong.

"Yes," he said, shoving his hands into the pockets of his slacks. She wondered if he knew doing that made the huge bulge pressing against his zipper more pronounced. "You're an excellent swimmer."

"Then I guess it's a good thing I decided not to ditch my bathing suit and swim nude."

He reached out and tucked a wet strand of hair behind her ear. "Yes, that was a good thing. But then again, I would not have minded seeing you swim naked, Paige."

Paige looked into the penetrating dark eyes staring back at her. "What time is it, Jess?"

He glanced at his watch, then back at her, and said, "It's close to one in the morning."

She nodded. That meant it was a brand-new day. Making up her mind about what she wanted and how she intended to get it, she tossed the towel aside and began stripping out of her bathing suit top.

"What do you think you're doing, Paige?" Jess asked in an incredulous tone.

"What does it look like?" she asked, removing her bikini bottoms and then stepping back so he could take in the view. "You said you wouldn't mind seeing me swim naked, and I'm ready to take you on, Jess Outlaw."

She quickly turned and got back in the pool.

Twelve

Desire slammed through Jess with a force that nearly knocked him to his knees. In the moonlight, Paige's naked body was total perfection as she stroked through the water. As she swam from one end of the pool to the other, his gaze followed her. It roamed over her ass each time it protruded gracefully to the top, and over her breasts that poked out of the water when she switched to the backstroke. He was mesmerized.

"Hey, aren't you going to join me?" she asked, pushing wet hair back from her face and treading water in the center of the pool. "Swimming is on my list of fun things. We might as well kick things off with a bang."

Bang? Why had she said that? Lust took over his senses. Desire consumed him. His libido reached an "I need her now" level, and his arousal reached a state of no return. By the time they parted ways at the end of the month, their sexual needs, wants and desire would be fulfilled.

After quickly removing his shirt, Jess's hands went to his zipper, inching it down. Then he slid his pants, along with his briefs, down his legs. He knew Paige was watching him, and he was glad that he was the man she wanted. Reaching down, he grabbed his wallet from his pants to retrieve a condom. It had been in his wallet a long time, so he checked to make sure it hadn't reached the expiration date. It hadn't, thank God.

He watched her as he sheathed himself before easing his nude body into the pool. If there was any uncertainty in her mind about his intentions, all doubt should now be gone.

"Come here, Paige."

She smiled and shook her head. "If you want me, Jess, you have to come and get me." She then swam to the far end of the pool, away from him.

Oh, so now she wanted to play hard to get? He had no problem going after her. Maybe now was a good time to tell her that not only had he been captain of his dogsled team, but he'd also been captain of his college swim team.

He glided through the water like a swimmer going for the gold, and it didn't take long to reach her. When she saw him getting close, she laughed and swam to the other side. Without missing a stroke or losing speed, he did a freestyle flip turn and caught her by the ankles. The capture was swift. The minute he touched her, even more desire rammed through him, to the point where water couldn't cool him down.

"I got you," he said, pulling her toward him and swimming with her in his arms to the edge of the pool.

When they reached the shallow end, her feet touched the bottom, and she circled her arms around his neck. "No, Jess, I got you and I'm ready for you." Then she leaned in and took his mouth.

Jess didn't resist, and their tongues mated as they feasted on each other's mouths like this would be the last time they could. She then wrapped her legs around his hips. He cupped her backside and eased inside her.

Knowing he was inside her body nearly pushed him over the edge, but he was determined to hang on. He had never made love to a woman in a swimming pool, but damn, he was going to make love to her here. After breaking off the kiss, he licked the side of her face when she leaned back against the edge of the pool, pressing their bodies more tightly together.

"I would have preferred our first time being in a bed, Paige," he whispered before licking the side of her neck.

The sound of her chuckle spiked his arousal again. "This is more fun and a new adventure for me. I've never made love in a pool before," she said.

"Neither have I," he said, taking her mouth again. The heat was on, and he was taking full advantage, no longer able to keep his desire in check. When she began kissing him back while moving her hips in earnest, he thrust hard into her. Then harder. He tried to tell himself to slow down, but he couldn't. Her moans and the way she moved her hips to their rhythm drove him on.

Determined not to be denied the taste of her breasts, he released her mouth to take hold of one nipple and suck hard, loving the taste. After a while he was convinced that he was addicted to her nipples.

"Jess!"

The sound of her screaming his name while grinding her hips against him pushed him totally over the edge. He could feel his neck enlarge as he was hit with a full-blown orgasm, the likes of which he had never experienced before. The intensity ripped from the top of his head to the bottoms of his feet planted solidly on the bottom of the pool.

He had been mesmerized by the beauty of her naked body moving through the water, but now he was totally captivated by this, the way her inner muscles clenched him as another orgasm tore through him and, from the reaction of her body, a second one consumed her as well.

"Paige!"

It seemed to take forever for the effects of their orgasms to pass. When his heartbeat had returned to normal, he pulled her close, knowing what they'd shared was an experience he would never forget. Even now, his greedy erection wanted to go for thirds when her inner muscles tightened on him again. That was the only condom he had with him, so he needed to get out of here so as not to put her at risk.

"We need another condom or two," he said, climbing out of the pool with her body still wrapped around him.

"Even three, four or more," she added excitedly.

He laughed. "I have more at my villa. We'll shower and then make love in a bed. Your villa or mine?"

She smiled, and unable to resist her lips, he kissed her. When he released her mouth, he put her on her feet.

"Doesn't matter to me," she said, sliding back into her bathing suit. "You've never been to my place, so the first time we try out a bed, it should be mine."

He chuckled. "Is that some kind of a rule?"

"Yes. It's the 'When on Vacation Rule Number Three.'"

He slid into his slacks and left off his shirt. Leaning in close, he brushed a kiss across her lips. "You need to tell me what rules one and two are later."

"Okay. Let the fun begin, and remember, what happens on vacation…"

"…stays on vacation," he said, pulling her close to his side as they headed back down the path.

Jess and Paige entered her villa and stripped naked. They rushed to the shower, and the moment they stepped inside, he pulled her into his arms and kissed her.

She would have thought they would be tired of locking lips, since they'd done it a lot of times tonight. Even when walking from the pool to their villas, they'd stopped every so often for their tongues to tangle. One time it had been so heated she thought he would haul her off to the nearest bench. He hadn't. But he had told her over and over again just how good her mouth tasted and how much he enjoyed savoring it.

When he released her mouth now, Paige couldn't help moaning her objection. She was still in awe of the feelings surging through her. Thanks to Jess, not only had she experienced her first orgasm, a second had followed close behind. She no longer wondered if she was one of those women unable to enjoy sex. Jess had definitely proved that notion wrong.

"Ready for our shower?" he asked in a husky voice against her moist lips.

"Yes, and, Jess?"

"Yes, baby?"

He licked around the corners of her lips, which made it hard for her to think straight. When she didn't say anything, he said, "You were saying, baby?"

Fighting back emotions stirring inside her, she said, "I have no problem with you being a sex-crazed guy. Right now, that's the kind of guy I need."

He stopped licking her lips to look at her. He had to be wondering why she'd said that. However, instead of asking her about it, he said, "I warned you earlier that I wouldn't be holding anything back. And, Paige, I meant it."

She doubted any guy had ever gone full speed ahead with her, and she couldn't wait to see what that entailed. From the penetrating look in his eyes, he didn't intend to give her any mercy. That thought made what little control she had left dissolve.

"Then bring it on, Jess," she whispered.

"Trust me—I will." Reaching up, he turned on the water and it sprayed over their bodies. Grabbing the tube of her shower gel, he squirted some into the palms of his hands and worked it into a lather before spreading it over her body. He lathered her chest, lingering on her breasts before moving to her stomach and legs and then upward to the juncture of her thighs. The moment he touched her there, she couldn't help but moan.

"You like my touch or the fragrance?" he asked as the scent of honeysuckle surrounded them.

"Both, but your touch takes top billing," she said, standing under the spray as she watched him cover the same paths on his own body. "I could have lathered you down," she said.

He shook his head. "No, Paige, you couldn't. I would not have lasted one second with your hands on me."

Before she could say anything else, he pulled her with him directly under the water to rinse the foam from their bodies. The warm water flowing over them felt divine. They were standing so close she could feel his erection.

"Now that we've gotten rid of that chlorine, let's concentrate on doing other things," he said, reaching out and pushing wet strands of hair from her face. "Have you ever made out in a shower before?"

His question made her blink. "Wh-what?"

He smiled. "Shower sex. I guess that means no. In that case, I'm going to make your first time one you won't ever forget."

The next thing Paige knew, Jess had dropped to his knees, buried his head between her legs and thrust his tongue inside her. The touch of his tongue on her clit made her weak in the knees, but his firm hands on her thighs kept her upright.

"Jess."

Her entire body nearly exploded when she saw, as well as felt, just what he was doing to her. Feelings she thought she was incapable of, especially to this degree, overwhelmed her. His tongue made her body writhe mercilessly against his mouth.

"What are you doing to me?" she asked.

He pulled his mouth away just long enough to look up at her and say, "Getting a good taste of you." Then he was back at it at full force, making her finally realize what all the hoopla was about.

She couldn't stop herself from gripping his shoulders hard when the sound of licking pushed her over the edge, making her hips tremble. She screamed his name. "Jess!"

He refused to let go until the last spasm left her body. Then he rose up, gathered her into his arms and whispered, "I've branded you with my tongue, Paige."

In all honesty, he'd done more than that, but she was too weak to tell him that, or anything else, for that matter. She whispered his name again. "Jess."

"I'm here, baby. Are you ready to dry off and get in bed?" he asked her while using the water nozzle to rinse them off again.

She nodded, and then he swept her into his arms and carried her out of the shower.

After drying them both off, Jess swept Paige back into his arms and left the bathroom to carry her to the bed. He had told her that he had branded her with his tongue. What he didn't say was that her flavor was now embedded in his taste buds, just like her scent was ingrained in his nostrils, for all eternity.

Not that he was counting, but he knew so far he'd given her three orgasms. He had felt them, tasted them and enjoyed them as much as she had. The only reason he hadn't made love to her in the shower was because he hadn't had a condom with him. The next time, he would.

He glanced around her villa's bedroom, seeing how much it resembled his. However, he noticed the primary baths were different. This villa had both a huge Jacuzzi tub *and* a walk-in shower. Whereas his only had a walk-in shower. However, he would say the shower in his villa was three times the size of hers. The next time they showered together they would use his. He imagined everything they could do within those four walls.

"You want me to get your nightgown?" he asked, when he noticed it thrown over the back of a chair.

"No, I want to sleep naked tonight," she said, easing under the covers. She smiled over at him. "Now you'll have to sleep naked, too."

Was that her way of inviting him to spend the night? Hell, he hoped so, because he didn't want to leave. "I don't have a problem with that. Let me lock up and I'll be back."

"Okay."

What he also needed to do was grab all those condoms he'd stuffed in the pockets of his slacks when they'd made a pit stop at his villa. With just a towel around his middle, he walked out of the bedroom and picked up their clothes from where they'd stripped out of them. After checking to make sure all the doors were secure, he went back into the bedroom. Glancing over at the bed, he saw Paige had dozed off. That was fine. She needed her rest and there was always morning.

After placing all the condom packets on the nightstand, he put his slacks on the same chair where she'd laid her nightgown. He then took her wet bathing suit into the bathroom and placed it in the sink. Going back into the bedroom, he then flipped off the light and eased in bed beside her. When he gently pulled her into his arms, she mumbled a few words in her sleep, but didn't wake up. He studied her face. Her lips were swollen from his kisses.

It had been a while since he'd gone to bed with a woman sleeping in his arms. She looked beautiful, peaceful. Like her, he should be exhausted. It would be daybreak in a few hours. But he couldn't sleep because their lovemaking had filled his body with combustible energy.

Never had he wanted a woman more and never had he been as satisfied after making love. But for him it wasn't just sex. He couldn't help but admire her for the recent decisions she had made. There was no doubt siding against her agent and standing up for herself wouldn't win her any brownie points in Hollywood. From the sound of it, Kemp was Hollywood's golden boy. Still, someone needed to school him on how to respect a woman, especially when that woman was supposed to matter to him. That was just common decency. Something Pierson evidently didn't have. What an ass.

Paige shifted positions, which brought them chest to chest. He could feel her breasts pressed against him and, instinctively, he entwined their legs. Not that he thought she was going anywhere, but he'd discovered how much he liked their bodies to be connected. Besides, just in case she woke up during the night, he wanted to be as close as he could get to her. He had wanted Paige the first time he'd seen her. It had taken six years, with regrets for him and a heartbreak for her before they finally got the timing right.

Whether she realized it or not, he'd done more than brand her. He'd staked a claim. By the time their vacation came to an end, she would know the place she had in his life.

Thirteen

The ringing of the phone caused Paige to open her eyes. She would recognize that ringtone anywhere. Why was Nadia calling her before daybreak? She opened her eyes to reach for her cell phone when she realized her legs were entwined with someone else's. That was when she recalled everything that had happened last night, at the pool and in the shower. She then recalled getting into bed naked after inviting Jess to join her. Obviously, he had.

"Here you are," a deep, husky voice said, close to her ear. She was then handed her cell phone. She looked into Jess's face and saw the morning stubble. She liked the unshaven look on him.

"Thanks." She then clicked on. "Nadia, why are you calling me so early?"

"Stop whining, Paige. It's after seven here, which means it's after six there. Most people are up and moving around."

Paige yawned. "Whatever. What do you want?"

"To tell you what the media is saying about you and Jess. Put me on speakerphone so Jess can hear, too."

Paige raised a brow and glanced over at Jess. He'd been staring at her, and their gazes connected. Immediately, her body responded like it had been a physical caress. Unable to look away, she then asked Nadia, "What makes you think Jess is here?" and put Nadia on speakerphone anyway.

"Honey, after seeing that kiss that has been seen around the world, I can't imagine him being anywhere else." Then, as if Nadia had known for certain Jess was there, she called out, "Good morning, Jess."

He smiled, and at Paige's nod, he said, "Good morning to you, too, Nadia. Now, what were you saying about my and Paige's kiss?" he asked, pulling himself up in bed and bringing Paige with him. The moment he touched her, frissons of heat raced through her body. That had never happened with a man's touch before. Only his.

"I said, your interview last night is all over social media. I even understand YouTube crashed from the number of people viewing the video of the two of you kissing. What you said, Jess, about letting Paige know just how taken you are with her, was so romantic, and then to follow it up with one of those tongue—"

"Thanks for calling to let us know our interview went over well, Nadia," Paige interrupted her sister to say. The last thing she needed was for anyone, especially Nadia, to describe the kind of kiss Paige and Jess had shared in front of those reporters. She knew just how magnificent it had been.

"Has Pierson made a statement yet?" Jess asked.

"Not yet. He's probably somewhere wiping mess off his face. Everyone expects him to say something since Paige pretty much contradicted his claim that the two of them were still together. You and Paige looked good together, Jess, like you belong to each other. Several papers said that as well. Twitter users think you using this time to go after Paige is so romantic, Jess, and the hashtag #Jessie'sGirl is trending. Also, #ReclaimingJessTime. There are some articles and posts suggesting you should be a top contender for Hottest Man Alive for next year, Jess," Nadia said.

Paige glanced over at Jess, and, amazingly, he only shrugged, like the thought of such a thing was of no significance to him. When Kemp had gotten the news that he was being considered for the title, he had danced around her bedroom for a full hour. Then he had called his agent to make sure all the proper interviews would be set up and necessary contacts made.

"If I didn't know better, I'd think the two of you aren't playacting and that Jess meant everything he said about being taken with you from the first and that the two of you are now making a go of it," Nadia said. "And that kiss. You can't convince me it wasn't real. Paige, you were as caught up as—"

"Thanks for the update, Nadia," Paige interrupted again. "I need to get up and get dressed now."

"Are you going to tell me why Jess is there with you this early?"

"No."

"Jess, will you tell me?" Nadia asked.

Jess chuckled and then asked, "How much is it worth to you?"

Paige gave Jess a warning look before throwing her hand over her eyes and grinning. Her sister was too much, and she didn't need Jess to encourage her. "Love you, Nadia. 'Bye." Paige then clicked off the phone and handed it back to Jess to place on the nightstand before she eased back down in bed.

After replacing the phone, Jess turned back to her and stretched his naked body alongside hers. If it was his intent for her to feel his erection, then he'd accomplished that feat. It felt hard, massive and definitely ready. "Good morning, Paige," he said in a deep voice while gazing at her with those penetrating eyes.

Why did he have to look at her like that? Doing so only made her remember their night in the pool and then later what he'd done to her in the shower. The memories were so vivid she could feel herself getting hot between the legs. "Good morning, Jess."

"Are you ready for our day to begin?" he asked.

Paige wasn't imagining it. His erection was getting even larger against her hip bone. "Yes, we're going jogging this morning and then breakfast, and later I will go with you to buy your paints," she said.

"Right."

"Just so you know, I'm having lunch with Chardonnay at the main house to follow up on my assignment."

"Your assignment?"

She swallowed. Was she mistaken or was his face moving closer to hers? "Yes. I told you I offered my help with her grandparents' anniversary party. My job is to follow up with those who haven't sent back their RSVPs. Most are those who might have forgotten. I'm calling them with a friendly reminder. That shouldn't take but a couple of hours."

"I see."

His face was now so close to hers that she could interpret the desire in his eyes and feel his breath on her lips. "What about you?"

"What about me?"

She groaned when he snaked out his tongue to lick one corner of her lips and then the other. His action nearly made her cry out his name. "What about me, Paige?"

She drew in a deep breath. "What will you be doing while I'm spending my time with Chardonnay?"

"I can use that time to make calls to set up some of our fun activities for the week. Hopefully, if I'm able to find all the supplies I need at the store this morning, we can have our first portrait session this evening."

"That sounds good." She was tempted to tell him his body close to hers felt good, too.

He shifted in bed again and his body moved even closer, nearly on top of hers. "But you know what I want to do now, Paige?"

She had an idea, but preferred that he tell her. "What?"

"This."

He took her mouth, showing her that he craved her taste as much as she craved his. Each and every time their tongues tangled, erotic sensations captivated her. No other man's kiss had the ability to do that. If this was what a "hot, romantic entanglement" entailed, then she was more than all in as long as Jess was involved.

He finally released her mouth and threw back the bedcovers to gaze at her naked body. Watching him look at her with such intensity and desire was one of the most erotic moments she'd ever experienced.

"Now I get to make love to you in a bed, sweetheart," he whispered in a low voice.

Reaching up to the nightstand, he grabbed a condom, and while she watched, he sheathed his huge erection. *Lordy.* She was amazed at how such a large penis could fit into such a small condom. But it had.

He looked at her and smiled before straddling her with a pair of muscled thighs. Then he closed his mouth over hers, kissing her with more deliberation than before. She heard her own moans, which meant he heard them as well.

Jess slowly broke off the kiss and eased back to stare down at her breasts, at the hardened tips of her nipples. She drew in a quick breath, marveling at how aroused she got just from knowing he was paying attention to a certain part of her body…and licking his lips while doing so.

Shifting, he lowered his head to her chest. Before she could pull in another breath, he had cupped her breasts in his hands and was devouring her nipples while gently kneading the firm mounds.

Her nipples throbbed mercilessly beneath the onslaught of his mouth, and she was convinced at that moment that her breasts were specifically made just for him.

Sensations swept through Jess as he sucked hard on Paige's nipples. Never in his life had he wanted to taste a woman so badly—to the point where he was filled with a sexual need so intense that her moans were nearly pushing him off the edge.

Trying to regain control, he eased back from her breasts and trailed kisses down her stomach and licked around her navel. Her taste was addictive. It unleashed an urgency within him to brand her again. Just in case he hadn't made his point last night.

Moving his lips farther south, he captured her womanly core, locking his mouth on her while tightening his hold on her hips. There was no doubt about it—he was definitely captivated by her taste. He was as hooked as any man could get. That had to be the reason a primitive urge had taken over his body as he greedily displayed, with his tongue, just how obsessed he was. Her moans were getting louder, and when her thighs began shaking, he knew what was coming. She was.

He barely had time to tighten his hold on her hips when she released a deep, wrenching scream that shook the rafters. However, he refused to let up. He continued to stroke her with his tongue while she writhed. He'd never known a woman who was as passionate, responsive and receptive as Paige.

When the last spasm left her body, he eased up to

straddle her and waited for her to open her eyes to look at him. His loins were about to explode with the need to get inside her, but he needed her to look at him. He needed the connection to her. So he held on to what little control he had until her eyes flickered open and met his gaze.

At that moment whatever he was going to say was lost as emotion caught hold of his senses. It left him speechless.

"Jess?"

Instead of answering her, he leaned in and took her mouth with a hunger he felt in every part of him. He finally released her mouth, mentally accepting all he was feeling. He lifted her hips and slowly eased into her. He watched her reaction as he did so, loving the sounds she made, which meant her body was ready again.

Slowly, with a measured pace, he pushed inside until he'd reached the hilt and couldn't go any more. As he drew in a deep breath, their scents were absorbed in his nostrils and total sexual awareness consumed him. Then he began moving, stroking the full length of himself in and out. Her response was immediate. Their limbs interlocked as he continued thrusting at a pace that was as deep and overpowering as it could get.

They were sharing perfect harmony. When she closed her eyes and moaned, thrashing her head from side to side, he increased the pace with every downward thrust. Over and over again. He felt it when her inner muscles took hold of him, clenched him, clamped down hard, but he kept going, refusing to let up.

Her movements matched his rhythm. His moans

matched hers, and he was driven to reclaim her mouth, mate with it while the lower part of him mated with her. Her taste fired his need, took control of his senses and pushed him over the edge. But he was determined to take her with him when he went.

The magnitude of his thrusts increased. He released her mouth and threw back his head as the veins in his neck nearly popped from pleasure. That was when he felt her body begin shattering beneath him, and it drove his to do likewise.

"Jess!"

The moment she screamed his name, he felt like everything was ripped out of him, pushing him into a universe of sensual bliss. He couldn't stop coming. It was as if his release was a nonending flow just for her. Gripping her hips, he continued to thrust hard, letting it rip, giving them both what they needed and wanted.

And at that moment he knew what it meant to not just have sex but to make love. He'd known it last night in the pool, and what they'd just shared reaffirmed that belief. Paige Novak had taken him to a place he thought he could never go again, and he knew there was no turning back.

Paige looked at herself in the vanity mirror, not believing how long she and Jess had spent in bed that morning. He had left an hour ago to go jogging without her. She'd been too exhausted. Instead, she had stayed in bed to rest up before her meeting with Chardonnay. That meant his painting would be delayed a day, but what they'd shared this morning—practically all morning—had been worth it.

She wasn't sure how many times they'd made love. More specifically, how many times he'd made her come. All she could say was it had been more than she'd ever done before, because until him, she hadn't done a single one. If her face was glowing, it was because Jess had given her something no other man had—total, absolute and complete sexual fulfillment.

Paige had, however, noticed several passion marks on certain parts of her body. Thankfully, none in places that could be seen by others. Jess had left a number of marks on the areas close to the juncture of her legs. Her body ached in certain places, but that didn't bother her. Instead, it was a wonderful reminder of what they had shared.

She had finally gotten up to get ready and was about to blow-dry her hair when her cell phone rang. It was Jill. She wondered if Nadia had told Jill about Jess spending the night. It didn't matter if she had.

Paige clicked on the phone. "Yes, Jill?"

"Don't 'yes, Jill' me. Everybody is talking about that kiss."

Deciding to play dumb, Paige said, "What kiss?"

"You know what kiss. And just so you know, according to the media, Kemp is scheduled to make a statement later today."

Paige rolled her eyes to the ceiling. "I honestly don't know what kind of statement he can make, unless it's to admit he screwed up and that we've both moved on."

"Well, all I've got to say is that you and Jess have

played your roles well. A lot of people believe your story."

Jill's words made Paige realize Jill hadn't talked to Nadia. "Have you spoken to Nadia today?" she asked.

"No. I see I missed a couple of her calls, but when I called her back, she was in a meeting. I figured she was calling to let me know about all the media buzz, so I checked for myself. Like I said, you and Jess have outdone yourselves."

Paige nibbled on her bottom lip before coming out and saying, "Jess spent the night, Jill. That kiss was real."

There was a pause, and then Jill said, "Seriously?"

"Yes, seriously."

"And what he told those reporters about letting you know how taken he is with you—that's real, too?"

"No, not that part. Just the kiss."

"Um, are you sure?"

"Yes. After that kiss we needed to explore all that sexual chemistry we're transmitting, but it's not that he is taken with me. We're both horny."

Jill burst out laughing. "That's too much information, Paige."

"Well, it's true. Our relationship is based on sexual pleasure and nothing else."

"Wow. And how do you feel, being the object of Jess Outlaw's attraction and receiving all that sexual pleasure?"

Paige couldn't help but smile. "Wonderful. Over the moon, thrilled with every part of my body."

"My goodness. So what's the rest of your plan?

You've started something and you better believe the media will keep up."

"Let them. Jess and I planned to do a lot of fun stuff on vacation, not for the media but for us. We figured we might as well enjoy our time here. We're going up in a hot-air balloon, bike riding, horseback riding and a lot of other stuff. Did you know he likes to paint?"

"No, I didn't know that."

"I didn't either. He showed me a picture that he did of Charm's mother, and he's good. He wants to paint me while I'm here. He intends to hang it in his place in DC."

"Seriously?"

"Yes."

"Um…"

"Okay, Jill, what's that *um* for?"

"I'm just wondering why Jess would want to hang a portrait of you in his home."

Paige rolled her eyes. "It will not be of me per se. It will be a painting of Napa Valley. He's using the vineyards as the backdrop."

"I don't care what you say, Paige. You'll be the main focus of that picture. No man hangs a woman's picture in his home unless she means something to him."

Paige shook her head. "You've been watching too many romantic movies, Jill."

"I think you need to keep your eyes open, Paige, for signs that Jess may honestly like you."

"He does like me. If I thought otherwise, I wouldn't be indulging in a vacation affair with him. But neither of us is looking for a long-term commitment. After

Kemp, the last thing I want is to jump back into a serious relationship with anyone."

Jill didn't say anything for a moment. "When Aidan and I first got involved, it was not supposed to be serious either, but..."

"But you ended up falling in love with him—I know."

"If you know it happened to me, then you should know it could happen to you, Paige."

There was no need to tell her sister that it had already started happening. She'd been falling for Jess for a while, and at some point, either last night in that pool or in the shower or in bed this morning, she'd accepted it to be true. It really didn't matter. The important thing was that neither she nor Jess was ready for that kind of a commitment. Her life was in Hollywood and his was in Washington. All they had and would ever have was what they were sharing now. Even so, she wasn't opposed to an occasional hookup whenever she saw him at family functions.

"Paige?"

"Yes?" Then, remembering what Jill had said, her response was "Jess and I know falling in love is not in the plan, Jill." She was speaking for him now and not for herself since it was too late for her. Jess didn't love her, and she accepted that.

"Still, my advice to you is to be careful and guard your heart. Westmoreland blood runs through Jess's veins, and take it from one who knows. A Westmoreland man is capable of capturing your heart even if you don't want it seized."

Knowing she needed to end her call with Jill before

she spilled her guts and told her sister how she really felt, she said, "Thanks for the warning, and I will be careful."

There was no need to promise to guard her heart. It was too late for that.

Fourteen

"You don't seem bothered by the comment Pierson has released, Paige," Jess said, glancing over at her as they walked from the main house back to their villas.

Paige's tasks for Chardonnay hadn't taken up as much time as she'd assumed they would, and they had gone into town to purchase the paint supplies he would need. After returning to the vineyards, they'd even gone walking and he'd shown her the area he had selected for the backdrop. She had agreed it was nice.

She looked up at him now. "Why would I be bothered? I can't control what Kemp says while he's trying to save face. He's the one who will look like a fool when the two of us don't get back together, Jess."

Jess didn't say anything as they continued walking. Paige hadn't seen Pierson's interview with the press a few hours ago, but he had. The man seemed pretty damn cocky, too sure of himself...and of her. He'd basically said he wasn't concerned about her starting a relationship with anyone because, in the end, he would be the man in her life.

"He's saying the two of you will eventually get back together. That you're just going through a moment," he told her.

Her chuckle should have been reassuring, but he honestly believed the man had gotten into his head that what he'd said was true.

"One thing I've learned about Kemp is that he's all into himself. Like I said, we won't be getting back together for any reason."

He heard what she was saying, and he hoped like hell she meant it. Why did it mean a lot to him that she did?

Jess suddenly knew the answer. He had fallen in love with her. Absolutely and irrevocably.

When had it happened? He wasn't sure. Could have been the first time he'd seen her six years ago. But he could say he'd first realized it while making love to her. Now there was no doubt. He was certain. As certain as she sounded about the end of her relationship with Pierson.

He looked down at their joined hands. He had taken hold of hers the moment they'd left the main house after dinner to walk to the villas. He liked touching her, and with her hand in his, they were a united force. He felt good about that.

"How's the guest list coming?" he asked.

"Great. Like I figured, most of the people planned

to come—they just hadn't taken the time to mail back their replies. There were a few who weren't home, so I left a message. I will follow up with them by the end of the week."

After a pause, she asked, "So what's on our agenda for tomorrow? My entire day is clear."

He glanced over at her. As usual, she looked beautiful in her yellow sundress. He'd noted she had worn flats. He hadn't realized just how short she was; however, in bed their bodies fit perfectly.

"I figured we could go jogging in the morning, then have breakfast with the family." He chuckled. "You heard Grammy Russell. She's making her red wine pancakes. I haven't had them before, but they sound delicious."

Paige smiled. "They are."

Unable to resist, he wrapped his arms around her shoulders and gently pulled her closer to him as they walked. This was much better. He liked the feel of their hips brushing as they continued their stroll.

"And then we have an appointment to go up in a hot-air balloon that includes lunch at one." He paused. "Then tomorrow night we're going dancing."

She looked up at him. "Dancing?"

"Yes. Spencer mentioned early today that there's a nice nightclub at his resort that's perfect for dinner and dancing, with a live band. How does that sound?"

A huge smile spread across her face. "Wonderful."

He doubted she knew how hearing her excitement made him feel. Although when they'd gone into town for the painting supplies they had encountered reporters, that had been before Pierson's press statement. It had been easy to say "no comment" or "Jess and I are enjoying our vacation" and leave it at that. Tomorrow the press would expect her to address what Pierson had said. Would she?

He had received a number of calls from his siblings. Like Nadia, they'd told him about the public's reaction to that kiss he and Paige had shared. All of his siblings believed it had been for show except for Garth and Maverick. Maverick claimed he knew a real kiss when he saw one.

They came to the fork in the road. One led to her villa and the other to his.

"It's still early," he said, turning her in his arms.

She looked up at him. "Yes, it is. We never did finish up that last bottle of wine, did we?"

"No, we didn't," he said, his gaze on her face before he cupped her chin with his hand.

"Do you feel like having company?" she asked.

If only she knew how much. "Yes. You're welcome to my villa at any time, Paige."

"And you to mine, but tonight I want to do yours."

And he wanted to do her. "Then let's go to mine, sweetheart."

They were out of their clothes the moment the door closed behind them. Very similar to the night after their swim. The only difference was that tonight they were wearing more clothes and undressing took longer. But it was time well spent. All Paige had to do was glance over to see Jess's naked body to know he was ready for her. Of course, it had taken him less time to undress, but from the way he was watching her, she could tell that he had enjoyed watching…especially when she had stepped out of her panties.

"Come here, Paige," he said in a voice that seemed to caress her skin. She recalled him making that same request last night in the pool. She hadn't gone to him then and wouldn't be going to him now. She rather enjoyed him coming after her.

She shook her head. "If you want me, Jess, then you come and get me," she said, walking backward toward the bedroom.

He nodded while his gaze roamed all over her. "I have no problem doing that."

"Then do it."

When he moved toward her, she took off and had nearly made it to the bedroom when he caught her from behind and whisked her off her feet and into his arms. Wrapping her arms around his neck, she smiled up at him. "You got me."

"And I intend to keep you," he said, dumping her in the middle of the bed and then joining her there.

It was on the tip of her tongue to say that she would love keeping him, but she refused to say that. She knew the score. She was one of his "do good" projects, and he was merely helping her out as a friend. But what if…?

She wiped that possibility from her mind. If anything, Kemp had shown her that long-distance relationships didn't work. All those months apart while filming had only deteriorated their relationship. And she would admit the distance between them hadn't been the only thing lacking with her and Kemp. The lack of sexual chemistry had been the main culprit. However, she had no such issue with Jess. All he had to do was look at her and she was turned on. Like she was now.

Not waiting for him to kiss her, she leaned in and kissed him. Jess was the only man Paige was convinced she could never get enough of kissing. His tongue was made to give pleasure, and it did so with such vigor and hunger, it caused her to moan. She was convinced she could reach a climax just from kissing him, especially if he continued to take her mouth the way he was doing now.

Jess held her in his arms so tightly that she could feel them skin to skin, flesh to flesh, with the tips of her nipples pressing against his chest. There was no way she could miss the feel of his engorged sex pressing hard against her thigh. He broke off the kiss, and the look in his eyes increased her desire for him.

Paige watched as he reached to the nightstand and opened the drawer to grab a condom packet, then ripped it open with his teeth. The hunger she saw in his gaze nearly undid her. He made quick work of sheathing himself, and then he was there, straddling her, and she automatically widened her legs for him. Cupping her hips tightly, while still holding her gaze, he entered her, filling her totally and completely. To her way of thinking, their bodies fit well together. Perfectly.

"Paige?"

She swallowed at the intense desire she saw in his eyes. "Yes?"

He opened his mouth as if he was about to say something and then he closed it. Instead, he began moving, making slow, long strokes at first, and then increasing the pace. He continued to hold her gaze, and she wondered what he'd been about to say. But at that moment words didn't matter—feelings did. And from the way he was staring down at her with heavy-lidded eyes, she was experiencing all kinds of feelings.

She grabbed hold of the strong forearms planted on both sides of her. Throbbing desire overtook her, and the feel of flesh sliding against flesh had purring sounds coming from her throat.

Her hands wrapped around his magnificent back and she felt the muscles bunch beneath her fingers with his every thrust. She decided that he wasn't the only one who could work muscles, and she began working hers, clenching him hard with her inner muscles, refusing to release him when he tried pulling back.

"Give it to me, Jess. All of it. All of you."

The lush shape of his mouth eased into a smile. "Are you sure you want all of me, Paige?" he asked with so much passion she could actually hear it.

"I'm positive."

He then leaned in and kissed her, taking her mouth with an urgency she felt all the way to her toes. This kiss was taking her on a high she'd never been on before and she intended to savor it. He sucked hard on her tongue as his thrusts went deeper, and she literally lost it. Her body jerked at the same time his did, and they both convulsed with desire.

He kept thrusting as sexual fulfillment ripped through

every part of her body. When he broke off their kiss, she screamed his name at the same time he hollered hers.

"Jess!"

"Paige!"

They both surrendered to the pleasure overtaking them. She called out his name again, drowning in the essence that was Jess. The taste, scent and feel of him were so sinfully erotic it took her breath away.

It did something else, too. It made her realize just how much she loved him. Not just for this, but also for the man that he was. She had dated enough to compare, and she concluded Jess was in a class by himself.

She settled into his arms as he held her, her cheek against his, and although he had no idea, her heart now belonged to him.

"That was some ride," Paige said the next day as Jess placed his arm around her shoulders, leading her away from the area where the colorful hot-air balloon had landed. "It was fun."

"I'm glad you thought so." He had enjoyed being with her as they glided across the valley, more than fifty feet in the air. Feeling her excitement the moment they'd boarded had been a high for him by itself. Then, standing beside her as they prepared for liftoff, he hadn't been able to stop his gaze from roaming over her in a pair of skinny jeans and a cute sleeveless top.

Every time he looked at her, he had remembered last night. She had spent the night in his villa, and that morning they had gone jogging and showered together. He doubted he would ever forget all the things they'd done in that shower. His shower was larger than hers and had a bench that he'd put to good use, making love to her while water streamed down on them.

"Jess?"

"Yes?"

"Do you want to stop somewhere to grab something to eat? We have a few hours before we start the painting session."

He had made dinner reservations for them at one of the restaurants in town before a movie. Tomorrow they would go bicycling in the countryside. Today he'd begin painting her and he was looking forward to it after getting all the art supplies he needed.

"What do you have a taste for?" he asked her.

She looked up at him. "Chardonnay told me about a place not far from here that sells the best hamburgers and fries. What do you think about that?"

His arm tightened around her shoulders, drawing her body closer to his. "That sounds great. Let's go."

Less than an hour later, they were sitting outside at a café that overlooked the valley while enjoying the best hamburger he'd ever eaten. Even the fries and strawberry milkshake were awesome. When he finished the first hamburger and ordered a second, Paige's eyes had widened. He had laughed and told her that he was a man who had a big appetite after all. Whether it was eating a meal or making love to her. His words had made her blush.

Jess liked seeing her blush. She'd done it a lot last night, and he'd said some pretty risqué things just to see that color come into her cheeks. It was obvious other men hadn't told her what they wanted to do to her, and how they would be doing it. He also liked surprising her and had done so with several positions she hadn't known were possible. He appreciated that she'd been open to new things.

There was so much sexual chemistry surrounding them. Did she feel it, too? He'd gotten turned on just watching her eat her burger and fries. And then the way she was sucking on her straw reminded him of when she had…

His phone rang and he released an annoyed sigh. The ringtone indicated it was his office back in Washington. They wouldn't be calling unless it was important. "Excuse me—I need to get this," he said to Paige, and then walked over to an area that would provide better phone reception. "This is Senator Outlaw."

"Senator Outlaw, this is Ron Overstreet. I just wanted to give you a heads-up that the Senate majority leader has indicated he might call everyone back to Washington to vote on an important bill next week."

Jess knew exactly what bill would be voted on, and it was important that his party seized the opportunity to make sure it passed. That meant everyone needed to be there for the vote. He glanced to where Paige was sitting as she sipped through her straw, gazing over the valley. The thought of leaving her, even for just a day or so, had him missing her already. "That's not a problem, Ron. Just keep me informed so I can make the necessary arrangements."

"Yes, sir."

When he returned to the table, Paige glanced over at him. "Everything's okay?"

"It depends on how you look at it." He then told her he might be needed back in Washington next week.

She nodded. "Duty calls. How long will you be gone, or will you even return here before the party?"

Was that disappointment he heard in her voice? He hoped so. That would mean she didn't want him to leave any more than he wanted to go. "No more than a day or so. Once the vote is taken, I'll be back. We still have a lot of fun things to do."

"When will you be leaving?"

"Not sure. Probably the middle of next week, if the majority leader can round up everyone by then. We're on vacation and everyone is in different places. Some of my fellow senators even made plans to leave the country, like Reggie. He's visiting Delaney in the Middle East. It won't be easy to get everyone back. However, we all know how important it is for this bill to pass."

She smiled over at him. "I'm going to miss you even if you're only going to be gone for a day or so."

"And I'm definitely going to miss you," he said, taking her hand and bringing it to his lips. "That means we need to have as much fun as we can before I leave."

Around them, they could hear the clicking of cell phones, which meant their picture was being taken. Jess didn't mind. He liked being photographed with her. "Are you ready for your painting session today?"

"Yes, but you haven't told me what to wear or if there is a particular color that will blend better with the background."

While still holding her hand, he leaned closer and whispered, "I would love painting you wearing nothing at all, Paige."

She threw her head back and laughed. "That wouldn't go over well if you still plan to hang it in your living room."

He smiled. "Art is art. However, I never said I would hang the picture of you in my living room. It's been my intention all along to hang it in my bedroom."

Jess saw surprise light her eyes. "Your bedroom?"

"Yes." There, he'd given her something else to think about. Before she could ask him about it, he released her hand and said, "It's time to leave."

Holding hands, they were walking toward their parked car when suddenly they were surrounded by a number of reporters. They were not surprised their location had been leaked when several people at the café had been taking pictures with their cell phones.

"Miss Novak, are you going to refute what Kemp Pierson said yesterday?"

Jess wrapped his arm around Paige's waist, as she smiled at the reporters. "Jess and I have been so busy enjoying our vacation that I have no idea what Kemp said," she said.

"He's saying that no matter what you've told us, it's all been a misunderstanding. Once he completes the filming of his movie and the two of you get a chance to talk, everything will be worked out."

Jess didn't say anything, but wondered how in the hell Pierson thought betraying Paige had been a "misunderstanding." He glanced over at Paige. Retaining her smile, she tilted her head as if giving the reporter her complete attention. She moved closer to Jess, and he tightened his arm around her even more when she said, "Regardless of what Kemp says, I think I've made it clear that I've moved on and therefore I really don't have any more to add. Good day, everyone."

Jess opened the car door. Ignoring the reporters throwing out more questions, she waved at them before he closed the door. One reporter then asked Jess, as he walked around the car to get in on the other side, "Senator Outlaw, do you feel like you're caught in the middle of a Kemp-Paige affair?"

Jess stopped. "No, not at all. I'm not caught in the middle. You all heard Paige. She has moved on, and it's unfortunate Kemp Pierson isn't doing the same thing." He was tempted to add "What man would continue to claim a woman who'd made it clear on more than one occasion that she didn't want him?"

He didn't know Kemp, had never met the guy, although he'd seen one or two of his movies. Jess always thought he was a good actor but was beginning to wonder about his attitude. When a woman made it plain that she had moved on, then a man was expected to move on. Then again, the man had made a costly mistake. If he loved Paige, then he would fight for her.

Was that what Pierson was doing? Fighting for Paige and hoping she would eventually forgive him? They *had* been together for almost a year, so there had been an investment in the relationship on both of their parts. Could the man truly regret betraying her? And if given the chance to wear down Paige's defenses, would she forgive him?

Ignoring other questions being thrown at him, Jess got in the car and drove off.

"Tilt your chin up just a little, Paige."

Following Jess's instructions, she did just what she was told as he stood behind an easel. She was convinced an artist's cape had never looked as good on any man. His expression was serious, his concentration intense as he painted her. She recalled what he'd said at lunch. He would hang the portrait up in his bedroom. Was he serious? Why would he do something like that? She had been about to ask when he suggested they leave the café. They were then overtaken by reporters, and she had given them the same response she'd been giving since Kemp's statement.

Paige figured a lot of people were probably wondering why Kemp was so determined to get her back. What Kemp was doing was changing the narrative. At least, he was trying to change it. Instead of people seeing him as the man who'd betrayed her, he was trying to get them to see him as the man determined to win back her love. Kemp didn't want her love, and she knew it was nothing more than a publicity stunt cooked up by his publicist. He was capable of turning any negative into a positive. Well, she intended to be his one failure.

"Whatever thoughts are making your brows wrinkle, Paige, get rid of them. Think of something pleasant," Jess said. His words made her blink, as she did as he instructed. Thinking of something pleasant meant thinking about him.

When they'd returned for lunch, they'd made time for a "quickie" in her villa. She had wanted more, but hadn't wanted to appear greedy. They only had two weeks left before their vacation ended and she wanted to stock up on all the memories of Jess that she could. Today had been her first quickie, but she didn't intend for it to be her last. It had been short but so darn enjoyable. He had cut through the foreplay and gone straight to the heart of the matter, and she had loved it.

"Did I tell you how much I like your outfit?"

Jess's words made her smile. "Thank you."

"That's it," he said in a husky voice, watching her before looking back at the canvas. "That's the smile I want to capture. The one I want to see every morning when I wake up and glance at your portrait."

Immediately, her full attention was on what he'd just said. "Why?"

He looked over the canvas at her. "Why what?"

"Why would you want to see my portrait every morning when you wake up?"

"Because I honestly can't think of seeing anything more beautiful."

His words made a lump form in her throat. "No more talking. I want to capture as much of the daylight as possible."

She didn't say anything else. Instead, she stared at him, giving him the expression he'd asked for. He'd told her to wear a blue dress. Not too dark and not too light. He wanted her hair down, flowing around her shoulders, and he wanted her to wear as little makeup as possible. She'd given him all he'd asked for, and when he'd seen her, he had said she looked perfect. Luckily, there was a bench for her to sit on, one that Spencer's men had placed there.

As she gazed at Jess, she focused on his mouth, that delicious mouth she loved whenever it connected to hers. Then, as he continued with swipes of his paintbrush, she saw how she was the focus of those deep, dark eyes. They had been at it for almost an hour, and she wondered how much longer today's painting session would take. She hadn't drooled yet, but if he continued to stand there while she visualized all that sexy, masculine body had done to her, she—

"Are you okay, Paige?"

She blinked. Her wanton thoughts had nearly overtaken her senses just now. She figured since he had asked her a question, it was okay to answer. "Yes. Why do you ask?"

"You look a little flushed."

Was that his way of saying she appeared hot? If only he knew. "How much longer?"

He tilted his head and looked at her. "Getting tired?"

She decided to go for total honesty. "No. I'm getting aroused sitting here looking at you, Jess."

Paige saw the way her words made his eyes darken, and then she watched as he placed the brush down and removed his cape before moving around the easel toward her. It was as if he was slowly stalking his prey and she couldn't move. She had no problem being an easy capture.

He offered his hand, and she took it. Then he drew her up close, and not for the first time, she thought they were a perfect fit. "You ever made love outdoors in the open?"

She shook her head. "No," she said, ensnarled by the look of passion in his eyes.

"Then let me show you how it's done." He swept her into his arms.

Fifteen

Paige sat in the huge Jacuzzi tub and soaked in the warm bubbly water. It had been another fun day. Over the past week they had gone horseback riding, had played strip poker a number of times—with her always losing—had helped pick grapes and had attended a wine tasting. And every day Jess would paint her. After that first day, she knew how each session would end. Jess said he was almost finished, but he refused to let her see any of it until it was completed. All he ever said was that, like he'd known, she was a beautiful subject.

That morning she had awakened in Jess's arms, and after making love they had showered together. After getting dressed, they had left her villa to drive to Windemere for breakfast and bike rentals. She didn't see as many reporters out and about. Since Kemp hadn't made any more comments, maybe they were no longer news. At least, she and Kemp weren't, but it seemed she and Jess were. Diehard romantics were still posting photos of them being seen together.

After breakfast, she and Jess had gotten on the bikes and ridden through several vineyards of Napa Valley. The terrain and scenery had been beautiful. They had taken a packed lunch—compliments of Grammy Russell—and had stopped to eat in front of a huge lake. She hadn't been on a bike in years and had enjoyed seeing the beauty of the land.

When they had returned to Russell Vineyards, they had showered and taken a short nap before going to play a game of tennis with Spencer and Chardonnay. It had been the battle of the sexes, and although the guys had won, Paige had totally enjoyed herself.

She and Jess had decided to make it an eat-in night where he would do all the cooking. Together they had gone to a grocery store in town to get all the ingredients he needed. There was an outdoor grill between the two villas, and they decided to use it.

But now she needed to soak. He had prepared the bath for her before getting a phone call. She wondered if it was the dreaded call to let him know he needed to return to Washington. She would miss him, but he'd said he'd only be gone for a couple of days and would return.

Paige definitely had something to do until he got back, like finally getting into that book she'd packed. She could envision herself hanging out by the pool and reading. It had been years since she'd taken time out for herself. It felt good to slow down and enjoy life, and thanks to Jess, she was doing that. Tomorrow they would be taking a wine-tasting class at the resort, and she was looking forward to it.

She tilted her head when Jess walked into the bathroom. She studied his features and knew, as she'd suspected, he had gotten the dreaded call. Funny how after having spent only weeks together she was able to read his expressions. He might have to leave, but she would definitely give him a good reason to rush back.

"Join me," she invited when he handed her a glass of wine. "This tub is big enough for the both of us."

He stood there for a minute as if thinking about her invitation. Then he sat on the edge of the tub to remove his shoes and socks. She drew in a deep breath as she watched him, and again her brain registered just how handsome he was. She recalled what Nadia had said some social media users were buzzing about. Jess Outlaw was a hottie, through and through. She would have to agree. There was more hotness in Jess's little finger than Kemp had in his entire body.

He stood, and she thought even now, while standing beside the tub fully dressed in a pair of jeans and a T-shirt, he looked gorgeous. Seeing him made her mouth water. That was why she decided at that moment to take a sip of her wine.

"And you're sure there is room in there for me?" he asked, glancing down at her. Bubbles totally covered her body, practically to her chin. He had prepared her bath and had gotten a little heavy-handed with her foaming bubble bath. Not only were there bubbles all over the place, the scent of honeysuckle filled the air.

"I'm positive, Jess."

"In that case…" His hands went first to his shirt and pulled it over his head before moving to the waist of his jeans to slowly ease down the zipper.

She watched his every movement. One thing she liked about her "hot, romantic entanglement" with Jess was how he turned each moment into a memorable experience. One that was fun in a way she'd never experienced before. And she was glad she was sharing it all with him. She would need these memories at the end of their vacation when he went his way and she went hers.

Looking up at him beneath her long lashes, she couldn't help the purr that flowed from her lips when he removed his jeans and briefs and stood there naked, displaying all his masculine and magnificent glory. The woman in her couldn't help appreciating the size of his manhood. She recalled the times she had fondled it, tasted it, kissed it.

"I need to pour my own glass of wine before I join you," he said, his words, along with his warm smile, awakening an achy hunger she felt all the way to her womb.

"Don't bother," she said, holding up her glass. "We can share."

His smile widened even more. "I'm fine with that," he murmured.

And then, after sheathing himself with a condom, he lifted one leg and then the other to join her in the tub. "Did I do this?" he asked, indicating all the bubbles, as he eased down in the water.

"Yes," she said, chuckling. "You were only supposed to put in one capful, but I think you put in four."

"Oh, well, I guess we'll both be squeaky clean in the end," he said, easing closer to her. "I like all this room we have in here. More room to play."

She thought so, too, and handed him her wineglass. He took it and placed it to his mouth for a sip. "I can't say enough how good Russell wines are."

"I can't either. I've already made plans to ship bottles to my home in California. Guess what all my friends are getting this Christmas?"

He then placed the wineglass to her lips for her to take a sip. Their gazes held. He hadn't mentioned what his phone call had been about and she figured he would verify her suspicions later. In the meantime, she wanted to enjoy every moment she could spend with him.

When he placed the wineglass aside, she knew he was ready to get down to business. He wrapped his arms around her, easing her close. So close that her nipples pressed against his chest, and she could feel his hardness between her legs. The water hadn't affected his length. If anything, his erection seemed to have lengthened to reach her.

They leaned in for a kiss at the same time, and the minute their tongues connected, the flames between them were already out of control. His tongue made all kinds of erotic movements in her mouth as he continued to stoke the passion blazing between them. This was the kind of kiss a woman could get addicted to, the kind that could leave its mark.

A part of her wanted to claim his mouth and tongue as hers, but she knew she couldn't do that. A "hot, romantic entanglement" was not meant to last. It was just for the moment, so she was definitely enjoying every second. Deciding to give just as much as she was getting, she gripped Jess's shoulders and slanted her mouth, needing as much of the wildness of his taste as she could get.

When he deepened the pressure, she couldn't help but moan. Suddenly, he broke off the kiss and she saw fiery desire in his eyes. "Turn your back to me, Paige."

Paige did what he asked, trying not to swish any water on the floor from the tub. He fit his body snugly behind her and used his hand to open her womanly folds before entering her. And then he began riding her, thrusting in and out, splashing water all over the place. But she didn't care. All that mattered was Jess and his ability to pleasure her so immensely.

When she began screaming his name, he tilted her head back toward him and covered her mouth to kiss the scream. Their tongues tangled again until he pulled his mouth away to holler out her name. Then he was kissing her again while turning her around in his arms, bracing her back against the tub, making sure she felt every stroke of his tongue.

Paige knew the one thing that was happening on this vacation was that Jess was branding her as his. Not a single place on her body was left unmarked. That might not have been his intention, but it was happening regardless.

"I'll be leaving Wednesday to return to Washington for a couple of days, Paige."

She opened her eyes and looked up at Jess. They had gotten out of the tub hours ago. After making love in bed, she was cuddled close to him and had been about to fall asleep. "I figured as much, although I was hoping otherwise," she said softly. "I'm going to miss you."

"I'll miss you, too. We'll have three days before then, and I'll be back in two."

She nodded. "And I'll look forward to your return." And she meant it. It would be crazy to tell him how she felt about him, though she would admit that tonight, while making love, she'd been tempted to. But she hadn't. She would keep her feelings to herself.

"Ready for dinner?"

Paige smiled at him. "Yes, since you are doing the heavy cooking. I'm just making the salad."

He chuckled. "There is nothing heavy about throwing a couple of steaks, potatoes and corn on the grill."

"If you say so."

He pulled up in bed and pulled her up with him. "You've never grilled before?"

She shook her head. "With all those male Westmorelands around who swore they were an ace when it came to grilling, there was no need. But just so you know, I'm starving. Thanks to you, I've worked up an appetite."

An hour later, they had gotten dressed and were outside. Jess had thrown on a couple of steaks and she'd come outside to keep him company. Later tonight they would go swimming again.

"I got a call from Pam. She said Crystal is doing fine with the babies and Bane is a big help."

"I bet he is. Now he has five sons and one daughter."

She glanced over at Jess. "What about you? Do you think you'd ever settle down, marry one day and have children?"

She might have been mistaken, but there was a look in his eyes that stirred emotions within her. Emotions that seemed to be flowing between them. She drew in a slow breath and figured she had only imagined such a thing.

"Yes, I plan to marry one day, and I do want kids. I'm not getting any younger. What about you? Marriage and kids in your future? Or are you planning to make your career in Hollywood your life?"

She took a sip of her wine as she thought about his question. "I don't plan to make Hollywood my life. In fact, lately, I've been thinking about getting out of acting and into teaching."

Paige could tell by his expression that her statement surprised him. "Why? You're good at what you do."

She smiled. "Thanks, but there are times I want the old Paige back."

"The one who was a rebel instead of a conformist?"

She was glad he had actually been listening to her that day. "It's not that I want to be a rebel, Jess. I just want to be me. Like I told you, Hollywood expects you to be who they want you to be. Pam tried to warn me, but I thought I was ready and could take them on and still be myself."

"And now?"

"And now I'm tired of thinking my image is all that matters, and that I should meekly go along with having my words scripted. Not sure I'm going to last in Hollywood, Jess." There was no need to tell him about that call she had gotten from Maxie, where this big producer had threatened to pass on her being in a movie for which she had been a top contender. Needless to say, her agent was not too happy with her now, especially with how Paige was handling the Kemp issue.

She paused and then added, "So to answer your question, yes. One day I want to get married and have children."

What she didn't say was that she would marry him in a heartbeat and have his babies. In just the short time she'd spent with him, she could see Jess being both husband and father material. He was thoughtful, kind, considerate and dedicated to those things he believed in. He was a good senator, and she could see great things in his political future.

"I think these are ready to come off the grill now," he said, breaking into her thoughts. She glanced over at the steaks. They liked theirs the same way, well done, and he was right. They were ready, and they smelled delicious.

"Are we playing cards after we eat?" she asked him.

"Yes. Strip poker. You game?"

She threw her head back and laughed. "Yes, Jess Outlaw, I'm game."

Sixteen

"I hate that you'll be gone by the time I get there, Jess, but I'll be glad to keep Paige company until you get back."

Jess paused while tugging on his slacks. He had placed Maverick's call on speakerphone as he got dressed. Now he wished modern technology was such that he could reach into his phone and pull his brother through it. He knew Maverick's comment was meant to get a rise out of him, so he would oblige his baby brother. "Cross the line with her, Maverick, and I'll kick your ass."

Maverick laughed. "Why, if I didn't know better, Jessup, I'd think you were jealous. But that's not possible since all you and Paige are doing is role-playing, or am I thinking wrong?"

"Think whatever you want, just remember what I said. And why are you coming to Russell Vineyards now when the party isn't for another week and a half?"

"I finished up the business I had in Ireland and returned to Alaska to find everyone was gone. I thought about flying to Wyoming to pay Cash, Brianna and the twins a visit, but decided not to wear out my welcome since I was there just last month. So I decided to fly to Napa Valley to hang out with you and Paige. Too bad you won't be there most of the time."

"I'll only be gone a couple of days, so don't do anything that will get you in trouble."

Maverick chuckled. "So warns the man whose face is all over social media. Do you know a group of women are trying to get your name added to the list of contenders for next year's Hottest Man Alive? I bet Kemp doesn't like that. I heard he'd planned on holding the title two years in a row."

Jess honestly didn't care anything about Kemp Pierson. He was glad the media was convinced Paige had moved on even if Pierson wasn't. A short while later, Jess had ended the call. After telling Paige he would be leaving today to return to DC, they had worked in all the fun they could within those three days. Thankfully, he had finished his painting of her.

He glanced at his watch. He would be leaving for the airport soon. They had spent last night together in his villa and had showered together this morning. She had left so he could pack and said she would grab breakfast for them to share before he left.

Jess didn't ever recall regretting leaving a woman, but he regretted leaving Paige. It didn't matter that he would be seeing her again in a couple of days. He had gotten used to spending time with her. Every waking moment. In and out of bed. He had gotten to know her, and she had gotten to know him. He'd never shared any details of his relationship with his mother to any woman, but he had shared them with Paige. He'd even talked with Paige about the bill he was flying back to Washington to vote on and why it was so important that it passed. She had listened, asked questions and genuinely seemed interested in what he had told her.

He heard the knock on his door. Upon leaving the bedroom, he moved through the living room to open it. Seeing Paige standing there with bags in her hands and a huge smile on her face made him miss her already. He had even thought of asking her to go to Washington with him, but knew she had promised to take on a couple more duties to assist Chardonnay with the anniversary party.

He stood back, let her in and then watched as she sashayed her delectable backside in a pair of shorts into his kitchen and placed the bags on the counter. By the time she had turned around, he was there, standing in front of her.

"Jess! Goodness. I didn't hear you move from the door."

He didn't respond. Instead, he pulled her into his arms and held her. "I'm going to miss you."

She pushed back to look up at him. "I'm going to miss you, too. Terribly."

Hearing her say that gave him hope. Hell, it gave him more than hope. It gave him enough motivation to say, "I think we need to have a long, hard talk when I get back. A talk about us, Paige, and where we want to go from here."

He held his breath, hoping she didn't say they didn't need to talk because they wouldn't be going any place from there. But she didn't say that. Instead, she said, "I will be looking forward to having that talk with you, Jess."

He released the breath he'd been holding and pulled her back in his arms, capturing her mouth with his.

"Have you heard from Jess?" Chardonnay asked Paige a few days later as they went over the final list of attendees. The caterers had to be notified of the exact number of those attending.

"No, but I did catch the news. It seems the senators are practically spending their nights at the capital, determined to push the bill through."

Chardonnay nodded. "That's what I heard as well."

They looked up when there was a knock on the door. "Janice, our housekeeper, is off today, and the kids started back to school this week. Spencer is out of town and everyone else is out in the vineyards, so I guess I need to get that," Chardonnay said, grinning.

When Chardonnay left the kitchen, Paige decided to pour another cup of coffee. She missed Jess like crazy and he'd only been gone for three days. A day longer than either of them had expected. That first day he had texted her a few times, but she hadn't heard from him since. She knew how busy he was.

He'd said they would talk when he got back and that the conversation would be about them. Was she crazy to hope he wanted more from their relationship than what they were sharing on vacation? That he would want forever like she did? Did he feel they had shared something special over the past two weeks? Something that was too meaningful to walk away from?

She had just refilled her cup when she heard Chardonnay return. "Paige, you have a visitor."

Paige's back was to Chardonnay, and when she turned around, she knew both surprise and shock covered her features. "Kemp? What are you doing here?"

The man who stepped forward looked nothing like the savvy, handsome Ralph Lauren model he used to be. Instead, the dark eyes—known to make his fans drool—looked tired. His clothes, which usually looked immaculate, appeared to have been slept in.

"Over the past twenty-eight hours I've been on six different flights to get here, Paige. We need to talk."

Before she could say anything, Chardonnay said, "I need to take care of a few things upstairs."

Paige watched her friend leave and then narrowed her gaze at Kemp, wondering what lie he'd told to get past the vineyards' security. "There's nothing we need to talk about."

"Please, Paige. I really want you to hear me out. I

flew all the way from New Zealand to come talk to you. At least please listen to what I have to say."

At the sound of voices out back, she figured Chardonnay's grandparents were returning. Letting out a deep breath, Paige said, "Fine. We can go to the villa where I'm staying. It's only a short walk from here."

"Thank you."

Jess glanced at his watch as the plane landed. The vote in the Senate had taken a lot longer than he had anticipated, with both sides trying to argue the point. In the end, the bill had passed. Everyone had reason to celebrate and some had done so. He had caught the first plane out of DC to return here.

He missed Paige like crazy and couldn't wait to see her again. He had called ahead for a rental car, and it should be ready. He thought about calling Paige to let her know he was flying back today but decided to surprise her. He couldn't wait to hold her in his arms again, make love to her, but more importantly, he wanted to talk to her, tell her how he felt.

A short while later, he was tossing his luggage into the trunk of his rental car when his phone rang. Recognizing the ringtone, he clicked on. "What's up, Maverick?"

"Are you still in Washington?"

"No. My plane landed in California fifteen minutes ago and I'm loading up my bags in the rental. Are you at the vineyards?"

"Not yet. I met this flight attendant at the airport,

and she invited me to hang out with her for a couple of days."

"Flight attendant? I thought you were flying your Cessna here."

All of the Outlaws, including Charm, had their pilot licenses. In addition to the huge company jet, they each owned a Cessna. Due to Alaska's very limited road system, one of the most common ways of getting around was by aircraft. Locals liked to say that more Alaskans owned personal planes than cars. Not to give the impression of being the rich kid on the hill, Jess kept his Cessna back in Fairbanks and only used it whenever he went home.

"I did. I met her at the airport when we were both claiming our rental cars. She was staying at a hotel in town and invited me to join her for a night, and I took her up on it. One night turned into two, but what can I say?"

His youngest brother really couldn't say anything. It was no secret in the family that Maverick kept his pants unzipped more than he kept them zipped. "I'm still at the hotel, but will drive over to the vineyards in an hour."

"I'll probably get there right ahead of you and will see you when you arrive." Then he thought of something. "On second thought, Maverick, just catch me sometime tomorrow."

"Tomorrow?"

"Yes, tomorrow."

He didn't want Maverick to interrupt the quality time he intended to share with Paige. More than anything,

Jess wanted to see her, and the first place he intended to go when he arrived was her villa.

"So what do you want to talk to me about, Kemp?" Paige asked the moment the door closed behind them.

"I owe you an apology about that situation with Maya."

"That situation with Maya..." Funny how he'd phrased that. "You've apologized already."

"Yet you won't accept my apology."

She placed her hand on her hip. "Yes, I've accepted your apology, but that doesn't mean we will get back together. You destroyed my trust in you, Kemp, and I refuse to be with someone I can't trust."

"Would you feel better if I told you that we found out how it got leaked to the press?" Before she could answer, he said, "One of the maids at the hotel was paid a lot of money to get those pictures."

Paige rolled her eyes. "And you're shifting blame on the maid for your failure to keep your pants zipped?"

He rubbed his hands down his face. "I just wanted you to know how those pictures got out there."

"Honestly, Kemp, do you think it matters? You betrayed my trust. That's what matters."

"And what about you and that senator? You couldn't wait to hook up with him."

"Don't bring Jess into this like I did something behind your back. I told you when you called from New Zealand that I was ending our relationship, that I was moving on, and I suggested you do the same."

He lifted his chin. "No woman has ever broken up with me before."

"Then consider me your first."

"I need us to get back together for my next movie, Paige. The investors aren't happy about the negative publicity I'm getting. Our agents are working out a deal. Just pretend we're back together until filming is over. That shouldn't be hard to do. It's not like you're really serious about that Outlaw guy anyway."

She lifted a brow. "And why wouldn't I be serious?"

"Too soon. There's no way you've gotten over me."

That hit a nerve. "For your information, Kemp, I got over you months ago. In fact, I had planned to break up with you next month when you finished filming and returned to LA. Things weren't working out with us."

Anger flared in his features. "You were planning on dumping me? Yet you're upset because I slept with Maya?"

"One has nothing to do with the other. You should have been committed to me and our relationship until we ended things, just like I was. You didn't know what I intended to do, yet you slept with Maya anyway. I might forgive, but I won't forget. With that said, I want you to leave."

"Leave? I just got here. I'm tired and need a shower. Can I shower and then crash here for a few hours, Paige? I'm so tired I can't think straight. I promise to leave after getting a few hours of sleep."

Shower? Grab a few hours of sleep? Here? He has to be kidding. "No! Absolutely not!"

"Please, Paige. I'm about to fall on my face."

She drew in a deep breath. He did look as if he would fall on his face any minute. "Where's Marv?" Marv was Kemp's bodyguard and he rarely traveled without the man.

"He's at the hotel. I told him I needed to talk to you privately and had him drop me off. I'll call Marv to come back and get me when I'm ready to leave, but I desperately need to at least shower and grab a few hours of sleep."

Paige released a frustrated breath and glanced at her watch. "Fine. I will give you three hours, Kemp, and then I want you gone. I'm leaving."

"Leaving for where?"

"That's not your concern. Just be gone in three hours." She then walked out of the villa.

She was about to head down the path to the main house, but then she figured Chardonnay had probably left to go get the kids from school. And this was the time of day that Grammy and Grampa Russell settled in for a nap.

Paige could walk down to the pool and hang out there, but three hours was a long time to wait for Kemp to leave. Her conversation with him had been downright exhausting and now she felt tired. She then remembered Jess telling her where he kept the key to his villa, in case she ever needed to get inside for something while he was gone.

She headed for Jess's villa. Before she took her nap, she would call Maxie. How dare her agent work with Kemp's agent on anything before discussing it with her? Locating the door key under the mat where Jess had said it would be, she opened the door to his villa. She went inside after placing the key back where she'd found it.

Seventeen

Jess pulled into the grounds of Russell Vineyards and brought the car to a stop in front of the main house. Spencer was out of town on a business trip, and since it was close to dinnertime, he figured everyone was inside preparing for the meal. The first thing he intended to do was see his woman.

His woman.

He smiled as he got out of the car. Yes, Paige was his, and when they had their talk, hopefully she would agree with that assessment. Without even bothering to get his luggage out of the truck, he quickly walked down the path to her villa. He'd discovered she liked taking a nap around this time every day and hoped she didn't mind being interrupted from her sleep.

The first thing he intended to do was kiss her. Then

he would make love to her. And later they would go out to eat and then return to his place or hers and talk before making love again…and again…and again. Like he'd told his brother, he didn't want to be interrupted tonight.

Jess even thought about borrowing Maverick's Cessna so he could fly her to Alaska, that part of the north where it snowed all year round. He would love surprising her and taking her on a dogsled ride. Maybe sometime after the party.

The thought of being alone with her in a cabin high up in the mountains of Alaska had him smiling. He would even take her to his home in Fairbanks. The thought of that made him smile even more. He had it bad. He was in love, and after ten years, it felt good.

He finally reached her door and knocked. When he didn't hear a sound, he knocked again since she was probably napping. When he still didn't hear anything, he decided, quite disappointedly, to just let her sleep. He would go back to the car and get his luggage, go to his villa and unpack while waiting for her to wake up.

He was about to turn to leave when the door was snatched open. He blinked. Standing in the doorway was a half-dressed man wearing only his briefs and a damn sleepy look on his face. He recognized the man immediately. Kemp Pierson. What the hell?

Jess frowned. "Where's Paige?"

Instead of answering him, the man rubbed a hand down his face before looking at him with a smug smile on his lips. "Paige is in bed. Asleep."

The man's words were like a slap. It hit so hard he took a step back. "In bed?"

Kemp Pierson crossed his arms over his chest. "That's what I said. I'm surprised at you, Senator. You're older than I am, so you should know never to mess with a woman on the rebound. In the end, she's going to get back with the dude her heart belongs to. Sorry. Better luck next time. Now, if you don't mind, your timing is lousy. But for me it's perfect since I'm going to wake up Paige so we can get it on again." He then slammed the door in Jess's face.

Jess just stood there, anger boiling through him. He raised his hand to knock on the door; he had something to say to Paige, but then he decided not to bother. She'd made her choice. What had happened to what she'd told him about moving on? All the man had to do was re-appear and she'd taken Kemp back after what he'd done?

Sucking up his pride, Jess turned and headed back down the path. Jess kept walking until he reached his rental car and got inside. There was nothing for him here. He would go back to the airport for a flight home to Fairbanks. Forget the anniversary party. He wanted to be as far from here as he could get.

He was halfway to the airport when his phone rang. It was Maverick. At first he wasn't going to answer, but then knew he needed to. Chances were, Maverick had arrived at the villa and discovered he wasn't there.

"Yes, Maverick?"

"I thought you said you would be here. Chardonnay said she hadn't seen you, although she saw a rental car parked in front of the house earlier. Why did you leave?"

He didn't say anything for a full minute. "Have you seen Paige?"

"No. Why?"

"When you do see her, try asking her why I left."

"Oh. Did the two of you have a disagreement about something?"

"Yes, I guess you can say that. As soon as I got back, I went straight to her villa, and a half-naked Kemp Pierson answered the door."

"What!"

"You heard me. The man was dressed only in his briefs and proceeded to tell me that he and Paige had gotten back together."

"He told you? What did Paige say?"

"I didn't talk to Paige. She was in bed asleep."

"And you believed him?"

"Look, Maverick, I don't want to talk about this. I'm on my way back to the airport."

"Why?"

"I decided to fly home to Alaska after all. You're welcome to use the villa I was using since I don't plan to return, not even for the party. I'll call Spencer and Chardonnay tomorrow and give them my regrets."

"You're quitting just like that? Without hearing Paige's side of things? That's crazy, man. What if Kemp Pierson was lying? Paige isn't Ava."

Jess rolled his eyes, remembering how Pierson had said his timing was lousy. It seemed that was the story of his life. "Look, Maverick, I don't need advice from you. The key to the villa is under the mat." He then clicked off the phone.

"...You're quitting just like that? Without hearing

Paige's side of things? What if Kemp Pierson was lying? Paige isn't Ava..."

As Jess continued to drive, Maverick's words kept ringing in his ears, and no matter what he did, he couldn't get them out. What if Pierson was lying? The man had certainly done nothing but lie during this entire ordeal, especially when claiming he and Paige would get back together. Had that been a self-assured man or an over-confident one? Or maybe one who enjoyed weaving his own tales?

Deep down Jess knew Paige was nothing like Ava, who had dumped him when her ex-boyfriend had come back into the picture. But what reason would Pierson have to be at her villa wearing nothing but his briefs, opening her door, if they weren't back together?

The only person who could answer those questions was Paige. She owed him an explanation, and dammit, he intended to get one. Making a U-turn at the next traffic light, he headed back to Russell Vineyards.

Paige came awake from her nap when she heard the sound of the villa door opening. It took her a minute to remember where she was. In Jess's villa, lying across his bed. She pulled herself up and remembered that episode with Kemp and glanced at her watch. His three hours were up, and he should be gone by now.

A huge smile covered her entire face when she heard the sound of movement in the living room. Jess was back! She quickly got off the bed and rushed out of the bedroom. "Jess!"

She frowned when the man who turned to look at her

was Maverick. Feeling disappointed, she said, "Oh, hi, Maverick. I thought you were Jess."

He leaned back against the door. "Why would you think I was Jess?"

She tilted her head to look at him, thinking he'd asked an odd question. "Because this is the villa Jess is using."

"And why aren't you at your own villa?"

She wondered what had gotten into Maverick. Usually he was the fun-loving, playful Outlaw. For some reason, he seemed awful serious today. "Because, if you must know, Kemp showed up."

Maverick crossed his arms over his chest. "Did he? And?"

And? What on earth was wrong with Maverick? Why was he looking at her funny? "And he wanted to talk, and we did."

"That doesn't explain why he's in your villa and you're here."

Paige was getting a little annoyed with Maverick's questions and his attitude. "Okay, Maverick, what's going on?"

He rubbed his hand down his face before crossing the room to stand in front of her. "Evidently, Jess got played."

"Played?"

"Yes. By Kemp Pierson."

Paige lifted a brow. "What do you mean?"

"Jess arrived a half hour ago and went straight to your place. Pierson answered the door wearing only his briefs and claimed the two of you had gotten together and that you were in the bedroom asleep."

"What! And Jess believed him?"

"Evidently, Pierson put on a convincing act because, yes, Jess believed him."

"The man is an actor, for heaven's sake." Now it was Paige who rubbed her hand down her face. "Where is Jess now?"

"On his way to Alaska."

Paige's jaw almost dropped to the floor. "You mean to tell me that Jess came back here, believed what Kemp said without talking to me and is now on his way to Alaska?"

"Yes."

Anger flared inside Paige. "Well, he undoubtedly doesn't think a lot about my character if he thinks I'd spend two weeks in his bed and then share a bed with Kemp when he shows up," she said, not caring if she was giving Maverick too much information.

Maverick shrugged. "He probably was quick to think that way because of what Ava did to him. Did he tell you about her?"

"Yes, he told me how she betrayed him with some guy."

"Did Jess tell you that guy had been her old boyfriend?"

Paige paused. "No, he didn't tell me that. But it doesn't matter. I am not Ava."

"Well, you were on the rebound when Jess got involved with you, and so was Ava."

Paige glared at Maverick. "I'm not on the rebound.

A woman can only be on the rebound if she's still emotionally attached to her ex."

"And you're not?"

"Heck no. I planned to break up with Kemp anyway. I was just waiting until we both finished our film projects to do it."

Maverick nodded. "I take it that Jess didn't know that."

"I saw no reason to tell him before telling Kemp. The only reason I'm even telling you is because I told Kemp earlier."

"Why is Kemp at your place?"

"When he got here, he was tired after six flights. After our talk, he asked if he could take a shower at the villa and grab a few hours of sleep. After seeing how exhausted he was, I told him that was fine and he needed to be gone in three hours. He said he would be and that his bodyguard would be coming back to pick him up. He should be gone by now."

"Not sure that he is."

Paige frowned. "Hell, he better be," she said, moving around Maverick and leaving Jess's villa. She didn't care that Maverick was right on her heels as she marched down the path to her own villa. After slinging the door open, she found Kemp sitting on the sofa, drinking a glass of wine and watching television.

He had the audacity to smile when he saw her. "Hey, baby. I was wondering when you were coming back." He then frowned when he saw Maverick and asked, "Who the hell is he?"

Without answering his question, Paige crossed the

room and stood in front of him. "How dare you give Jess the impression that you and I were back together?"

Kemp shrugged nonchalantly. "He believed it, so what does that tell you about him?"

Refusing to entertain his question with an answer, she said, "Leave, Kemp. Your three hours were up a while ago."

"Leave? Why should I leave now that you and the senator are no longer together? We need to sit down, talk and work out our problem." He glared over at Maverick and then looked back at her and said, "Privately. I had Marv bring my luggage since I'll be staying awhile. Our fans are counting on us working through this, sweetheart." He glared at Maverick again. "And you haven't said who this guy is."

"Don't worry about who I am, asshole," Maverick said with a lethal tone in his voice, moving around Paige.

Paige touched Maverick's arm. "I got this, Maverick." She then turned to Kemp. "Your things are here?" she asked coolly.

He smiled. "Yes. I've unpacked most of them. And this is some pretty good wine," he said, holding up his glass. "I can't wait to meet your cousins-in-law who own this vineyard."

Paige fumed. As far as she was concerned, Kemp was an overconfident ass. He honestly thought he was staying. Without saying anything, she went into the bedroom and headed straight for the closet where she figured Kemp had hung his designer suits and hand-tailored shirts. Grabbing them in one huge sweep, she marched back to the living room, right past him and opened the door.

That got Kemp off the sofa real quick. "What do you think you're doing?"

Instead of answering, she tossed out the armload of clothing. And like she figured he would do, he rushed out past her to gather his expensive clothing off the ground. By then she had gathered the rest of his stuff and dumped them on the pile with the rest.

Down on his knees gathering his clothing, Kemp stared up at her in shocked disbelief. Maverick was laughing while taking photos of the entire thing with his cell phone. Unbeknownst to the three of them, Jess had walked up the path and was a witness to it all.

Eighteen

Jess would have thought the entire thing comical if Paige didn't have some explaining to do. At least, he thought she did, until she screamed at Pierson, saying, "How dare you insinuate to my boyfriend that you and I were sleeping together? I wouldn't waste my time sleeping with you again, especially now that I know what it's like to be made love to by a man who knows what the hell he's doing."

Something bloomed to life inside Jess. Had Paige just referred to him as her boyfriend and insinuated that Pierson was lousy in bed? All in the same breath? And from what she'd just said, Kemp had lied about them being together in her villa.

Before Pierson could say anything, Paige kept on talking. "Like I told you, I had planned to break up with you anyway, but you convinced yourself I still wanted you. What part of the words *I have moved on* didn't you understand? We are through, Kemp. I told you that three weeks ago. If you needed to hear it in person rather than on the phone, now you've heard it. Leave!"

Something must have given his presence away. Suddenly, Paige glanced over to where Jess was standing, and the glare she gave him was just as fierce as the one she'd been giving Pierson. Then she looked beyond him and her eyes widened. He turned around and saw the photographer at the same time bulbs from the man's camera flashed several times.

"No! No! Stop! I didn't want you to take any pictures now," Pierson bellowed out to the photographer, who only grinned while taking a few more shots before he dashed off to a parked car.

Paige glared back at Kemp Pierson. "You invited a photographer here to take pictures?"

Pierson glared back at her. "Yes, I invited him. He was to take photos showing we were back together."

Placing her hands on her hips, Paige scowled down at Pierson. "We are not together. I have moved on, and I suggest you do the same, Kemp."

Jess felt the intensity of her anger with him when she cut her scowl from Pierson and leveled it on him before walking around Maverick to go inside her villa and slam the door shut.

Maverick was rolling with laughter while Kemp Pierson was still on his knees in the grass trying to pick up all his belongings, mumbling about how much all the stuff cost. Suddenly, Paige's door flew open, and she tossed out Pierson's designer luggage.

"Wait, Paige. Baby. Can we talk? I didn't mean to make you mad," Pierson said, pleadingly.

She slammed the door shut, and that made Maverick laugh even more. Jess had seen and heard enough. He strolled up the walk to where Pierson was trying to put his clothes into his luggage. "When you finish with that, do as Paige said and leave."

Jess turned and moved toward Paige's door, but Maverick put a hand on his arm to stop him. "I wouldn't tangle with her right now if I were you, Jess. Give her time to calm down. She's pretty pissed at you for believing what that asshole said. She's hurt that you didn't trust her. The only thing you have in your favor is that you didn't fly home to Alaska, which hopefully means you thought about it and began doubting Pierson's story."

Maverick was right. He had begun doubting Pierson's story. "Where was she when Pierson was at her place?"

Maverick grinned. "She was at yours. In *your* bed taking a nap. Imagine what I thought when I walked into your place and this very attractive, sexy woman, with a mane of thick brown hair and drowsy sable eyes, sauntered out of your bedroom looking gorgeous as sin and delectable as any meal I could claim to have ever eaten."

Jess glared at his brother. "I imagine you were thinking she was off-limits and that your brother was a damn lucky fellow."

"I wouldn't count yourself lucky, Jess. Not until Paige forgives you." Maverick then put his cell phone in his pocket. "Had I known Pierson hired a photographer for this show, I wouldn't have bothered getting my own flicks."

Jess looked at Pierson, who was still on his knees in the grass gathering up his belongings, and shook his head. "Damn. How much stuff did he bring?"

"From the looks of it, a lot. Probably planned a lot of photo ops. Obviously, he honestly thought he could sweet-talk Paige into letting him stay awhile," Maverick said, chuckling. "Even I know a man should never be overconfident when it comes to a woman."

Jess eyed his brother. "If anyone should know, you would."

Maverick smiled. "Of course." He then glanced at his watch. "I suggest, while Paige is cooling off, that we go to your place for a beer, Jess."

Paige had stepped out of the shower and dried herself off when her phone rang. The ringtone indicated it was Nadia. Grabbing her phone, she clicked on, placing her sister on speakerphone when she slid into her caftan. "Yes, Nadia?"

"I can't believe you tossed Kemp and all his stuff out the door," Nadia said, laughing.

Paige lifted a brow. "How do you know about that?"

"Girl, it's all over social media, with pictures of Kemp on his knees in the grass gathering all his stuff. The tagline says 'When A Woman Tells You That She's Moved On, Believe Her.' The Twitter hashtag is #KempOutJessIn."

Paige rolled her eyes. "Whatever."

"So, what happened to bring out the wicked witch in you?"

Knowing Nadia would harass her until she told her, Paige sat on the edge of the bed and told Nadia everything, starting with when Kemp had shown up in Chardonnay's kitchen.

"And he made it seem as if the two of you were in bed together when Jess returned? But actually you were at Jess's villa in his bed?"

"Yes. All Jess had to do was to leave my place and go to his villa to find me and see Kemp was lying. Instead, he left to return to the airport to fly home to Alaska."

"Yes, but he did come back after he thought things through," Nadia rationalized.

Paige frowned. "He should not have left in the first place. Jess, of all people, should not have believed Kemp. I told everyone, including Jess, that I had moved on, and he should have believed me."

"Well, I'm sure Kemp was pretty convincing."

Paige rolled her eyes again. "Of course he was convincing. The man is an actor. Jess should have seen through the lie. He should have trusted me, and he didn't."

"Well, it sounds like you and Jess need to talk."

"I don't want to be bothered by Jess, Kemp or anyone else right now. I'm still mad."

"Well, don't overdo your madness and let a good man get away."

"A man who doesn't trust me."

"Where were Spencer and Chardonnay when all this action was going down?" Nadia asked.

"Spencer is out of town, and Chardonnay's parents arrived in town and she and her family were having dinner. She didn't know what had gone on until Kemp's bodyguard arrived to pick him up. That's when I told her the entire story, and like you, she had a good laugh."

"Well, everyone is laughing at those pictures. If nothing else, I think you got your point across to Kemp. And the no-nonsense women of the world applaud you."

After her call with Nadia, Paige got other calls—Jill, Pam and several members of the Westmoreland family. Even Delaney called from the Middle East. It seemed the incident had made world news. Spencer even called from Seattle to make sure she was all right and said he would find out how Kemp, his bodyguard and the photographer got on the grounds of Russell Vineyards. He wasn't happy about that. Paige had a feeling a few heads would be rolling.

Chardonnay was kind enough to send dinner to her by Russell. After eating, Paige sat at the table and drank a glass of wine. That photographer had taken those pictures mere hours ago, yet he'd wasted no time putting them out there. Kemp's plan to have a photo op showing them back together had backfired on him. It served him right.

Her thoughts then fell to Jess. She should have appreciated that he had come back and hadn't flown to Alaska, but then, why should she? He should have trusted her. He should have known she would choose him over Kemp any day.

But then, why would he think that way when he had no idea how she felt about him? He had no idea that their "hot, romantic entanglement" had turned into something she wanted to last forever. But still...

She glanced over at her door when she heard a knock. She had a feeling it was Jess. Should she answer it or not? She was still pissed. But in his defense—and she would admit he did have a defense—he was clueless about how she truly felt. They hadn't had that talk they were supposed to have when he got back. So for that reason, she would at least listen to what he had to say.

Moving from the kitchen table, she walked over to the door and looked out the peephole to make sure it was Jess and not Kemp returning. She honestly hoped he got the picture this time.

It was Jess, and as if he'd known she was looking at him, he stared back. She felt a deep stirring in the pit of her stomach. Frustration and desire were doing a serious dance inside her right now. Taking a deep breath, she braced herself and opened the door. He had showered and changed out of the slacks and shirt he'd been wearing earlier and was now dressed in a pair of jeans and a pullover sleeveless muscle shirt that showed off those forearms and shoulders she liked so much.

Forcing that thought from her mind, she tried to keep her face void of expression when she said, "Jess, what are you doing here?"

"It's time for us to have that talk, don't you think?"

At that moment she honestly didn't want to think *or* talk. He was staring at her with more than an assessing gaze. His close scrutiny made her feel downright carnal. How could a mere look from Jess do more than a touch from Kemp ever could?

Even now, he had every hormone in her body sizzling. The intensity of his gaze caused her entire body to react, which prompted her to say, "You believed I could leave your bed and then sleep with Kemp, all in the same week."

The reminder of what he'd thought gave her a chill, but even that wasn't strong enough to quench the heat she felt with his dark eyes staring at her. "I'm sorry about that, Paige. May I come in so we can talk about it?"

She wasn't sure she wanted to accept his apology. She should close the door on him to let him know he was no more welcome into her space than Kemp. But she knew that wasn't true. It was this thing between her and Jess that had been there from the first, and they both knew it. Was she willing to turn her back on it now? No, but she wasn't about to make things easy for him. She would listen to what he had to say and then decide what direction she would take.

Instead of answering him, she took a step back. The moment he entered and closed the door behind him, she visualized all the other times he had walked into this villa. She was convinced that over the past two weeks they had made love nearly everywhere in her villa and his. And she had not one regret about it.

When he turned to face her, she asked, "So why are you here and not in Alaska, since you intended to put as much distance between us as you could, Jess?"

Jess shoved his hands in his pockets and met her gaze. He hoped she would listen to what he had to say.

He loved her, and more than anything, he wanted to convince her of how much. "I came back because I realized I let my emotions overrule my common sense."

Paige shrugged. "Well, I'm not sure returning here did any good."

"I want to think the opposite. Can we sit down and talk?"

She didn't say anything for a minute. "Okay then, let's talk."

He followed her to the living room and watched her ease down on the sofa as he sat in the wing-back chair facing her. She was watching him expectantly. What could he say to make her understand just how he'd felt at the thought of her reuniting with Kemp?

"I told you about my last serious girlfriend, Ava. What I didn't tell you was the guy I found her sleeping with was her ex-boyfriend. She had broken up with him less than a year before she and I got together."

She waved her hand dismissively. "I know that. Maverick told me earlier. What I don't understand, Jess, is what that has to do with me."

Could she not see the connection? "When I got here and Pierson told me the two of you had gotten back together, for me it felt like déjà vu. He sounded believable and I panicked when I should not have. It was only when I was halfway to the airport that something Maverick said made sense."

"What did Maverick say?"

"He reminded me that you weren't anything like Ava."

"So, it took another man to tell you what, as far as I'm concerned, you should have known?"

She was right. "I would have figured it out on my own, Paige—I had fallen in love with you so hard that I couldn't think straight."

She sat up straight in her seat. "What did you say?"

He had no problem repeating what he'd said. "I said I had fallen in love with you so hard that I couldn't think straight."

She tilted her head and looked at him. "You love me?"

"Yes."

"Since when?"

"Probably since the first time I saw you. If you recall, I told you the Westmoreland House held sentimental significance for me because of you. I'm convinced that's when I fell in love with you."

While she looked like she was in shock, he continued, "For years I saw the night I met you as a missed opportunity. When Dillon introduced us and I saw that flirty little gleam in your eye, I knew I had to put the brakes on or I'd be in trouble. That night I made a decision to choose a career in politics over starting something with you that I couldn't finish. A part of me has regretted it ever since."

"What are you saying?"

"I'm saying what I told those reporters that night at Sedrick's was true, Paige. What I've tried to do these past weeks was to let you know just how taken I am with you. The only reason I didn't let you know six years ago was the timing. Like I told those reporters, I was knee-deep in my campaign and intent on staying focused."

"But what about the other times, after you won your Senate seat?" she asked.

"I thought the time would be right, but you were either off filming or I was trying to get settled in Washington. When I had finally made up my mind to make my move, that's when I heard you'd become involved with Kemp Pierson and everybody was saying it was serious."

"It should have been, but it wasn't," she said softly.

"My time spent with you here was meant to recapture that missed opportunity, but what I really wanted to do, Paige, was to capture your heart the same way you had captured mine."

When she didn't say anything, just stared at him, he continued, "I didn't expect to pull things off in four weeks or less. I was planning to part ways with you at the end of our vacation, but I had hoped spending time with me would be so enjoyable that we could continue seeing each other."

"You never told me any of this, Jess."

"No. I never told you because I didn't want to rush you. I was operating on the assumption that you were trying to get over a broken heart. A woman on the rebound."

She let out a frustrated sigh. "If I hear that word *rebound* one more time I will scream. Like I told Maverick, I'm not, and never was, a woman on the rebound. I was never emotionally attached to Kemp after we broke up because I had planned to call it quits between us anyway. I was just waiting until we both finished our film projects to do it."

"So, in other words," Jess said, "Kemp's affair gave you an excuse to do what you'd planned to do anyway, which was to end things between the two of you."

"Yes, but regardless, he should have remained faithful to me until we mutually ended things. He didn't, and I had every right to feel betrayed."

"I agree."

She paused and then said, "I wish we would have had this talk sooner, Jess. Then you would have known that I fell in love with you that night six years ago as well. I told myself I was just attracted to you and the attraction would fade, but I would dream about you often. Things didn't go well for me and Kemp on so many levels. He was so full of himself, so overconfident in his abilities, that he never noticed how unhappy I'd become."

Jess leaned forward in his seat. "What are you saying, Paige?"

"I'm saying that I love you, too. I am at a point in my life where my career doesn't mean as much as it once did. If you recall, I even told you I was thinking about leaving Hollywood. I want to teach drama at one of the universities."

He captured her hands in his, not believing their talk had brought them to this point. Now, like her, he wished they would have had it sooner. She loved him and he loved her. "You do know there are performing arts departments at Howard University, Georgetown and George Washington University."

She smiled at him. "Any reason you mention those three that are located in DC?"

"Yes." He stood and pulled her from her seat and into his arms. Looking down at her, he said, "I just happen to know someone who would love seeing you more often."

She wrapped her arms around his neck. "How often?"

"How about every night and every morning? I love you, Paige."

"And I love you."

He then captured her mouth before sweeping her up and heading for the bedroom.

Epilogue

"For a while I thought I would have to send a search party out for you two," Maverick said, grinning at Jess and Paige when they walked into the anniversary party. It was obvious his gaze was drawn to the huge diamond on the third finger of Paige's left hand. He lifted a brow. "Is there something I need to know?"

A huge smile covered Paige's face. The day after their "talk," Jess had convinced her to fly with him to Alaska, high in the mountains near the Yukon and Arctic Ocean. A friend of his was the sheriff of this small town where it snowed all year round. His purpose for taking her there was for her first dogsledding experience. He had borrowed Maverick's plane to fly them there.

Jess pulled her closer in his arms and smiled at

his younger brother. "Yes. We had a great time in the mountains, Paige loves dogsledding and I brought your Cessna back in one piece."

Maverick frowned. "Cut the BS, please. That diamond on Paige's hand is almost blinding me. Do you want to tell me about it?"

Paige giggled and held out her hand. "We're engaged!"

Maverick lifted a brow. "Engaged?"

"Yes. We're getting married on Paige's birthday in late November," Jess said.

"November? That's three months from now," Maverick said.

Paige smiled. "Yes, three months, five days and approximately thirty-nine hours, but who's counting?"

Maverick laughed. "Damn, just what happened on that mountain, so I'll know never to take a woman there?"

Paige gave her future brother-in-law a cheeky grin. "Don't you know what happens on vacation..."

"...stays on vacation," Jess finished. "We will talk more later—it's time for us to mingle."

And they did. The Westmorelands and Outlaws were there in full force, and news spread quickly of an upcoming wedding in three months. Another Novak was marrying a Westmoreland cousin. Everyone was excited and happy for the couple.

"So, are you moving to Hollywood or is Paige moving to DC?" Dare Westmoreland wanted to know. Dare and his wife, Shelly, lived near Atlanta, where Dare was the sheriff of College Park, Georgia.

"We'll be living in both places until Paige finishes all her film projects. Then she's moving to DC," Jess said, smiling down at his fiancée.

"That's wonderful," Shelly said. She then glanced beyond them to see more guests arriving. A huge smile touched her face. "I see our son is getting a lot of attention."

Everyone followed Shelly's gaze and settled on AJ Westmoreland, Dare and Shelly's oldest son, who was the spitting image of a younger Dare. In other words, he was handsome as sin.

"That's AJ?" Paige asked, surprised. "Or should I say Alisdare," she added, since everyone had gotten word that nowadays he preferred being called by his birth name. "I haven't seen him in years. Last time was when he graduated from high school, and we all went to the graduation."

"Alisdare finished college with a bachelor's degree from the University of Maryland and a master's from Harvard, both in criminology," Dare said proudly. "Earlier this year, he was hired by the FBI. He wants to work a few years as an agent before joining his cousins at the Westmoreland Security Firm." The Westmoreland Security Firm was run by Dare's cousins, Cole and Quade Westmoreland. Cole, who was a former Texas Ranger, and Quade, who'd worked for PSF, a special unit of the Secret Service protecting the president, had started a network of security companies that was in thirty of the fifty states.

The seventy-fifth wedding anniversary party for Daniel and Katherine Russell was well attended and turned out to be the fabulous affair Chardonnay had wanted it to be. Pam and Dillon didn't make the event. They were busy back in Denver helping out Bane and Crystal with their two sets of triplets. Pam and Dillon had been the first Paige and Jess had called to give them their good news.

It took a while before Jess and Paige had a moment alone. He pulled her into his arms as they stood outside and gazed up into the sky.

"It's a beautiful night, isn't it?" she said.

Jess turned to Paige. "As beautiful as the woman I intend to marry. I love you, Paige."

Paige smiled up at him. "And I love you, Jess."

When he pulled her into his arms, Jess knew this had ended up being the best vacation ever.

* * * * *

Don't miss a single story in the
Westmoreland Legacy: The Outlaws series
from award-winning and bestselling author
Brenda Jackson!

The Wife He Needs
The Marriage He Demands
What He Wants for Christmas
What Happens on Vacation...

And Maverick's and Charm's stories,
coming soon!

WE HOPE YOU ENJOYED
THIS BOOK FROM
♦ HARLEQUIN
DESIRE

*Luxury, scandal, desire—welcome to
the lives of the American elite.*

Be transported to the worlds of oil barons, family dynasties,
moguls and celebrities. Get ready for juicy plot twists,
delicious sensuality and intriguing scandal.

6 NEW BOOKS AVAILABLE EVERY MONTH!

#2869 STAKING A CLAIM
Texas Cattleman's Club: Ranchers and Rivals • by Janice Maynard
With dreams of running the family ranch, Layla Grandin has no time for
matchmaking. Then, set up with a reluctant date, Layla realizes he sent
his twin instead! Their attraction is undeniable but, when the ranch is
threatened, can she afford distractions?

#2870 LOST AND FOUND HEIR
Dynasties: DNA Dilemma • by Joss Wood
Everything is changing for venture capitalist Garrett Kaye—he's now the
heir to a wealthy businessman *and* the company's next CEO. But none of
this stops him from connecting with headstrong Jules Carson. As passions
flare, will old wounds and new revelations derail everything?

#2871 MONTANA LEGACY
by Katie Frey
After the loss of his brother, rancher Nick Hartmann is suddenly the
guardian of his niece. Enter Rose Kelly—the new tutor. Sparks fly, but with
his ranch at stake and the secrets she's keeping, there's a lot at risk for
them both...

#2872 ONE NIGHT EXPECTATIONS
Devereaux Inc. • by LaQuette
Successful attorney Amara Devereaux-Rodriguez is focused on closing
her family's multibillion dollar deal. But then she meets Lennox Carlisle,
the councilman and mayoral candidate who stands in their way. He's
hard to resist. And one hot night together leads to a little surprise neither
expected...

#2873 BLACK TIE BACHELOR BID
Little Black Book of Secrets • by Karen Booth
To build her boutique hotel, socialite Taylor Klein needs reclusive hotelier
Roman Scott—even if that means buying his "date" at a charity bachelor
auction. She wins the bid and a night with him, but will the sparks between
them upend her goals?

#2874 SECRETS OF A WEDDING CRASHER
Destination Wedding • by Katherine Garbera
Hoping for career advancement, lobbyist Melody Conner crashes a
high-profile wedding to meet with Senator Darien Bisset. What she didn't
expect was to spend the night with him. There's a chemistry neither can
deny, but being together could upend all their professional goals...

HDCNM0322

*To oust his twin brother from the family company,
CEO Samuel Kane sets him up to break the company's
cardinal rule—no workplace relationships. But it's Samuel
who finds himself tempted when Arlie Banks reawakens
a passion that could cost him everything...*

Read on for a sneak peek at
Corner Office Confessions
by USA TODAY *bestselling author Cynthia St. Aubin.*

A sharp rap on her door startled Arlie out of her misery.

"Just a minute!" she called, twisting off the shower.

Opening the shower door, she slid into one of the complimentary plush robes, then gathered the long skein of her hair and squeezed the water out of it with a towel before draping it over her shoulder.

Good enough for food delivery. She exited the bathroom in a cloud of steam and pulled open the propped door.

Samuel Kane's face appeared in the gap.

Only he didn't look like Samuel Kane.

He looked like wrath in a Brooks Brothers suit. Jaw set, the muscles flexed, mouth a thin, grim line. Eyes blazing emerald against chiseled cheekbones.

"Oh," she said dumbly. "Hi."

A sinking feeling of self-consciousness further heated her already shower-warmed skin as he stared at her.

"Do you want to come in?" she added when he made no reply. She stepped aside to grant him entry, catching the subtle scent of him as he moved past her into the hallway.

"Why didn't you tell me?" he asked.

Arlie's heart sank into her guts. There were too many answers to this question. And too many questions he didn't even know to ask.

"Tell you what?" she asked, opting for the safest path.

Coward.

Samuel stepped closer, her glowing white robe reflected in icy arcs in his glacier-green eyes. "About my father. About what he said to you this morning."

The wave of relief was so complete and acute it actually weakened her knees.

"Our families have a lot of shared history," Arlie said. "Not all of it good."

"He had no right—"

"I'm sorry," she interrupted, knowing it was a weak and deliberate dodge. She didn't want to talk about this. Not with him. "It's absolutely mandatory that you surrender your tie and suit jacket for this conversation. I'm entirely underdressed and frankly feeling a little vulnerable about it."

Walking into the well-appointed sitting area, Samuel shrugged out of his suit jacket and laid it across the chaise longue. As he turned, they snagged gazes. He gripped the knot of his tie, loosening it with small deliberate strokes that inexplicably kindled heat between Arlie's thighs.

"Better?" he asked.

On a different night, in a different universe, it would have ended there.

But for reasons she could neither explain nor ignore, Arlie padded barefoot across the space between them.

"Almost." Lifting her hands to his neck, she undid the button closest to his collar. Then another. And another.

To her great surprise and delight, Samuel wore no T-shirt beneath.

Dizzy with desire, Arlie tilted her face up to his. The air was alive with electricity, crackling and sizzling with anticipation. The breathless inevitability of this thing between them made her feel loose-limbed and drunk.

"All my life, I could have anything I wanted." Cupping her jaw, he ran the pad of his thumb over her lower lip. "Except you."

Arlie's breath came in irregular bursts, something deep inside her tightening at his admission. "You want me?"

Samuel only looked at her, silent but saying all.

His wordlessness the purest part of what he had always given her.

The look that passed between them was both question and answer.

Yes?

Yes.

Don't miss what happens next in...
Corner Office Confessions
by USA TODAY *bestselling author Cynthia St. Aubin.*

Available May 2022 wherever
Harlequin Desire books and ebooks are sold.

Harlequin.com

Get 4 FREE REWARDS!

We'll send you 2 FREE Books plus 2 FREE Mystery Gifts.

FREE
Value Over
$20

Both the **Harlequin® Desire** and **Harlequin Presents®** series feature compelling novels filled with passion, sensuality and intriguing scandals.

YES! Please send me 2 FREE novels from the Harlequin Desire or Harlequin Presents series and my 2 FREE gifts (gifts are worth about $10 retail). After receiving them, if I don't wish to receive any more books, I can return the shipping statement marked "cancel." If I don't cancel, I will receive 6 brand-new Harlequin Presents Larger-Print books every month and be billed just $5.80 each in the U.S. or $5.99 each in Canada, a savings of at least 11% off the cover price or 6 Harlequin Desire books every month and be billed just $4.55 each in the U.S. or $5.24 each in Canada, a savings of at least 13% off the cover price. It's quite a bargain! Shipping and handling is just 50¢ per book in the U.S. and $1.25 per book in Canada.* I understand that accepting the 2 free books and gifts places me under no obligation to buy anything. I can always return a shipment and cancel at any time. The free books and gifts are mine to keep no matter what I decide.

Choose one: ☐ **Harlequin Desire**
(225/326 HDN GNND)

☐ **Harlequin Presents Larger-Print**
(176/376 HDN GNWY)

Name (please print)

Address   Apt. #

City   State/Province   Zip/Postal Code

Email: Please check this box ☐ if you would like to receive newsletters and promotional emails from Harlequin Enterprises ULC and its affiliates. You can unsubscribe anytime.

Mail to the Harlequin Reader Service:
IN U.S.A.: P.O. Box 1341, Buffalo, NY 14240-8531
IN CANADA: P.O. Box 603, Fort Erie, Ontario L2A 5X3

Want to try 2 free books from another series? Call 1-800-873-8635 or visit www.ReaderService.com.

*Terms and prices subject to change without notice. Prices do not include sales taxes, which will be charged (if applicable) based on your state or country of residence. Canadian residents will be charged applicable taxes. Offer not valid in Quebec. This offer is limited to one order per household. Books received may not be as shown. Not valid for current subscribers to the Harlequin Presents or Harlequin Desire series. All orders subject to approval. Credit or debit balances in a customer's account(s) may be offset by any other outstanding balance owed by or to the customer. Please allow 4 to 6 weeks for delivery. Offer available while quantities last.

Your Privacy—Your information is being collected by Harlequin Enterprises ULC, operating as Harlequin Reader Service. For a complete summary of the information we collect, how we use this information and to whom it is disclosed, please visit our privacy notice located at corporate.harlequin.com/privacy-notice. From time to time we may also exchange your personal information with reputable third parties. If you wish to opt out of this sharing of your personal information, please visit readerservice.com/consumerschoice or call 1-800-873-8635. **Notice to California Residents**—Under California law, you have specific rights to control and access your data. For more information on these rights and how to exercise them, visit corporate.harlequin.com/california-privacy.

HDHP22

Love Harlequin romance?

DISCOVER.

Be the first to find out about promotions, news and exclusive content!

 Facebook.com/HarlequinBooks

 Twitter.com/HarlequinBooks

 Instagram.com/HarlequinBooks

 Pinterest.com/HarlequinBooks

You Tube YouTube.com/HarlequinBooks

ReaderService.com

EXPLORE.

Sign up for the Harlequin e-newsletter and download a free book from any series at **TryHarlequin.com**

CONNECT.

Join our Harlequin community to share your thoughts and connect with other romance readers!
Facebook.com/groups/HarlequinConnection